SEEKER'S QUEST

Book Two of the Seeker's Trilogy

Cassandra Boyson

CassandraBoyson.com

DEDICATED TO

CailieEllen

CONTENTS

❧ I ❧

THE MOMENT IVIANA felt the life pass from the Realm Leader of the Greater Archipelagos, she prepared for Tragor's arrival. She knew the dragon would come for her within the day. Luckily, she hadn't unpacked much from her former travels. In fact, she had avoided the travel bag altogether, hesitant to confront any reminders of that world, the land in another universe. She feared the longing to be with the friends she had left behind would be too much if she revisited the things she had brought with her from the Greater Archipelagos.

As it was, Iviana was happy in Kierelia, something she had not been previously, though she had not known it in the years of her childhood. She had friends in the FairGlenn village now and she had created a simple, peaceful life. It was all she ever wanted, or it had been before she'd befriended a

1

dragon who had taken her to another realm. Furthermore, she'd defeated a sorceress who planned to destroy that land and found its next Realm Leader That leader happened to be her good friend Flynn who, too, had originally lived in Kierelia.

Iviana realized he would take his place as Realm Leader now Rhimesh had passed. It was foolish she had not anticipated his reign would come so soon, though she had known Rhimesh would not last forever. A sickness had invaded her body that no one had been able to fully heal, not even Iviana, though she had done what she could in an effort to lengthen her life.

These thoughts plagued her mind for hours as she awaited Tragor's arrival. But upon first sight of her dragon, the worries and mourning of the day ceased, if only for a short time, as she reacquainted herself with her old friend.

Iviana met him deep within the forest, for this had been their secret place when Tragor had stayed with her for a time. Dragons were considered an enemy of the land, thanks to the dark dragons created by the late sorceress, Aradia. Those dragons were known for the devastation they left in their wake and, though Tragor was not a dark dragon, the villagers had no way of understanding that. They had no idea dragons originated from another universe and had been tame at one time, before a number of them had been deceived by the sorceress.

As she entered the large clearing, Iviana looked the dragon over as he did the same with her. It seemed all they desired was to take in the sight of one another, for they had missed each other more than either could have anticipated. Iviana wondered if the strength of their bond was due to the fact that each had been a recluse for years until they had found one another. She, because the world had thought her a witch and he, because he had long ago lost his best friend, Iviana's great-grandfather, Latos. Iviana supposed this was what had attracted Tragor to her, for he must have noticed some similarity between she and her great-grandfather, some kindred essence, though Iviana had never known the man.

At last, a smile broke upon Iviana's face as she raced toward Tragor and threw her arms about his neck. He nuzzled his head against hers and enfolded her in his wings. The tears that sprang to Iviana's eyes startled her and she quickly brushed them aside before he could see her weakness. Though she knew better than to believe Tragor saw tears as weakness—he had certainly seen her cry before—somehow, after only several months apart from him, sudden timidity overtook her and she was ashamed that he should see her tears.

As she pulled away, he offered a long, curious look, gazing into her eyes until she allowed a few happy tears to spill from them. It was then he appeared content. It seemed he would allow no bashfulness between his favorite human and himself, for Iviana knew he was a very old dragon, even called ancient, his title being the Great Dragon of the Ages. In his old age, he did not feel the embarrassment that the young so often do. Moreover, he was a dragon and, as far as Iviana understood, dragons did not feel shame as humans do, or at least not often.

When at last they concluded their greeting, Tragor impatiently gestured to his back and Iviana admitted it was time they were on their way. Her goal was to arrive in the Greater Archipelagos by early morning before anyone was awake. She wanted to take her first steps on the Isle of Dragons privately, as she couldn't help feeling nervous about meeting her friends again after the way she had left. She would need time to gather herself.

The flight was even more exhilarating than she had remembered. It had been some time since she had soared through clouds with Tragor. This, she had dreamed of often in the late hours of the night. There was surely no experience to match it that she had yet to discover and, though Tragor proceeded with a little showing off upon noting her excitement, they succeeded in arriving in the Greater Archipelagos just before the first rays of the sun peeked over the horizon.

They had used the portal in the sky, of course, as it was the portal used only by dragons (the only creatures who had the strength to fly high enough to reach it). Iviana wondered, just as she had previously wondered in times before, just how they were able to reach the twinkling stars in order to enter the swirling vortex that served as a portal between Kaern and the Greater Archipelagos. But this was not something anyone had been able to explain, a mystery yet unsolved. Still, despite its altitude, dragons covered the distance in a matter of minutes due to their unmatchable strength and speed. Indeed, Iviana often found it difficult to breathe during the rush and it was always a relief to arrive on the other side of the vortex.

As Tragor soared over the Isle of Dragons, Iviana sleepily surveyed the island where her friends lived—the friends she had abandoned some time ago. Gracefully, Tragor rested on a beach further from where she needed to be than was convenient, but he understood her desire for privacy as she reacquainted herself with the place.

Bidding Tragor a reluctant farewell, Iviana made her way inland until she had reached the village. Silently, she tip-toed through a series of huts, praying no one would stir. But as a long whistle sounded from a nearby window, she winced. Looking to where she had heard it resound, she realized it had come from the hut assigned to the leader of the realm.

Before she had time to fully register this, a familiar face popped up from beneath the windowsill. "If it isn't the mysterious dragon savior, come to grace us with her long-awaited presence," Flynn said happily, leaping through his first floor window.

"You really shouldn't be whistling at strange women," Iviana scolded, reaching to embrace him. At least with Flynn, she did not have much guilt over the way she had left, for he had been the only one to whom she had informed of her leaving for Kaern.

"Oh, you're not so strange," he replied.

"That's not what I hear. Last time I spoke with Leilyn, I was told I needed to work on myself or I'd never catch a man."

Flynn bellowed a hardy laugh. "Well, I say we

leave the Seeker as is. I wouldn't have anyone to tease otherwise."

Before Iviana could warn him she did not want her presence made known yet, Flynn caught another early riser passing and asked him to inform Nimua and Naii that Iviana had arrived. Immediately the islander set off.

"He's obeying you?" Iviana questioned as they walked.

Flynn immediately sobered, his face grim. "What brought you here, Ivi?"

"Something's wrong. Something is wrong with Rhimesh?"

"Not 'wrong.' She is with the Great One and, according to the beliefs of our people, I believe that must be more than pleasant. I'm afraid the realm is left unsteady in the hands of its current leader, however."

"I disagree," Iviana said with meaning.

"Thank you. I wish I felt as confident, but I'm glad you're back. I could use your input."

"My input? I'm just—"

Flynn chuckled halfheartedly. "Just what? The woman who defeated Aradia? The one who recognized my call and brought me here in the first place? I hope you're not 'just' or I may have made a mistake in coming."

His words filled Iviana with inexplicable confidence, almost more than was natural. "Fine. But as I recall, I didn't face Aradia alone. There was an ornery fellow with me. Oh, and I had a dragon...and the Great One really did most of it...How's your gift coming along, by the way? Shouldn't you be using it to speak life over *yourself*?"

"Eh, being a Speaker isn't as easy as it sounds...it's complicated. You have to believe what you speak for your words to have power. Also, you have to be very, *very* careful what you say..."

"I've thought of that. It's a huge responsibility."

"No more than anyone else, I suppose...just different."

They walked quietly for a time before Flynn asked, "You know how Rhimesh passed?"

"I believe so. I think she wanted to go, though. She was ready. I mean, she's had the responsibility of Realm Leader for a long time. I know it wasn't as long as some of the past Realm Leaders, but the job must have been terribly tiring, nonetheless."

"Yes," Flynn agreed, turning a shade paler.

"She believed in you, Flynn. She didn't have to, but she did. You are chosen by the Great One for this position and you should ask Him what He would like you to do with it."

"Ask Him? I don't think it's that easy. I'm not a Seer; I don't know how to hear His voice."

As they approached Iviana's old hut, she took hold of Flynn's hand. "As you say, I am here to help. Perhaps we can discover the voice of the Great One together."

Flynn tightened his grip on Iviana's hand as if it was a lifeline, then dropped it. "I'll let you head in. I'm sure you'll want to freshen up before seeing everyone."

"Is that a hint? Have I got dirt smeared across my face or something?"

Flynn laughed. "No, but you looked alarmed when I asked that boy to tell Nimua you were here. I assume you'll want a moment to yourself."

Iviana smiled. "You know me well. I'll see you soon?"

Flynn nodded and went on his way.

Surveying the building that had previously been like a home to her, Iviana breathed deeply, readying herself for what she would find within. Since Flynn hadn't said anything, she gathered no one was living in it at present, but that didn't mean it had not been used in all the time she had been away. Throwing the door open, she expected to find it transformed back into the guest house it had once been, but was astonished to discover everything was just as she had left it. The only indication anyone had been in was the lack of dust and cobwebs. Iviana raced to her bedroom and was pleased to find it still decorated in hues of green and brown and flourishing with plant life. It appeared someone had taken care of the plants, even replaced a few, and her tody bird remained where she had left him, obviously taken care of with a clean cage and fresh food.

The little table in the corner of the room held an unfamiliar sheet of paper. Dated the day she had left for Kaern, it was proof of her ownership of the hut. Someone had pulled some strings and given her the property...on the very day she had left. Falling into the nearest chair, Iviana released a sigh. She did not regret having left, but wished she hadn't done so without saying goodbye.

Suddenly, a face she knew well appeared in the doorway, looking upon her with joy written on his face.

"You're back," Darist said with quiet relief.

Iviana smiled. "I am." Her smile faded, "I'm sorry I—"

"Don't feel badly, Ivi," he interrupted. "We knew you would return eventually. We're far too charming to abandon forever."

Iviana laughed and made her way across the room to embrace him. "Thank you, Darist. It's good to know you kept faith in me."

He nodded. "That paper on the table states this place is yours now. It belongs to you alone."

Iviana nodded. "I gathered that. Who—"

"Naii, Nimua and I. We spoke with the council, requesting they award the property to the girl who had brought the one chosen by the Great One to become the next Realm Leader of the Greater Archipelagos. You hadn't any home to officially call your own and we thought you would be remaining with us. Even so, it is yours."

Iviana made ready to begin another apology, another declaration of regret, but Darist grinned and spoke before she could continue, "I hope you don't mind, but I sort of managed the place while you were away. Kept it clean...kept that poor bird alive."

A blush flooded Iviana's cheeks. "I guess I hadn't thought about him when I left...it's a wretched thing to have done."

"Not as wretched as leaving without saying goodbye, you horrid girl," Nimua interrupted, surprising the two with her sudden appearance in the doorway.

Iviana looked at her friend in shame. "Oh, Nimua, I'm so sorry! I was stupid and—"

"Never-mind all that. Just get over here and let me hug you."

Iviana couldn't fathom how forgiving they were, but as warm as their mercy made her feel, she couldn't help wishing she could go back and leave the right way. At the time, she'd been afraid they would try and stop her. Moreover, she had been fearful their efforts would prove successful. She had been determined to leave before her fear of returning to a life that had formerly been painful consumed her. At any rate, there was nothing she could do to change it now.

The three caught up on all that had happened in while they had been apart. Iviana shared how the Great One had changed the way the FairGlenn villagers saw her and all the various ways life in Kierelia had changed. They, in turn, filled her in on the details of Rhimesh's cremation and burial the evening before, the traditional treatment for those who had passed on. It seemed it had been a beautiful ceremony, as Rhimesh had been well-loved by all. The law stated that the realm should be in mourning for the two months following the death of a Realm Leader, but they were sure to mourn her loss for years longer. In truth, the three sitting in Iviana's hut were certain the woman would never be forgotten.

Iviana grieved she had not been there for the burial service. She had hoped the proceedings following her death would not be so swift, but deaths were handled just as swiftly in Kierelia, so she was not surprised. Still, she planned to visit the burial site and honor the woman who had been a friend to her. Even when most of the islanders had not trusted her, Rhimesh had offered her a chance and that was all she had needed.

Iviana was thinking on this while Nimua and Darist discussed the funeral, when Nimua suddenly turned to her with an intrigued expression, asking, "So, Ivi...you know how Marquen never comes down from his hill to be with our people?"

Iviana looked at her with new interest and nodded.

"Well...he finally did."

"Really?" Iviana queried.

"It seems, just before her death, Rhimesh told the Healers she needed to see him...and he actually went. Well, really, how could he not? I mean, she was so ill. Anyway, he won't tell anyone why she wanted to see him and it's made the council very upset. They're threatening to banish him."

"There have been no threats," Flynn stated as he strolled through the patio door.

"Oh, but I heard—"

"Rumors. There have been no threats. Nor are there going to be. Yes, some are extremely angry with him, but it makes no difference. There are enough of us on the council who want him left alone."

The four spent hours catching up until Flynn was forced to return to the council hall for a session and Nimua insisted they go with him so Iviana could catch Naii before she entered the meeting. Iviana did not hesitate to consent, for Nimua's mother had been something like a mother figure or aunt to her and Iviana wished to see her as soon as possible, though she was nervous concerning what Naii would say about the way she had left.

There was no need for anxiety, however. Naii approached her with teary eyes and contented heart, simply pleased she had returned. There was no mention of Iviana's abrupt and unannounced departure—not even the smallest scolding—and Iviana could not imagine ever leaving them again. Even if the rest of the island was not pleased by her arrival, she had wonderful friends to support her.

After Naii was forced to enter the council hall,

Iviana asked that Darist and Nimua allow her a little time apart from them before the evening banquet so she could visit Marquen and see if she could wriggle the story about his meeting with Rhimesh. Nimua had consented more than graciously, for she was even more curious than Iviana.

When at last Iviana had completed her trek up the mountain that led to Marquen's cabin, she found him relaxing against the door-frame with arms crossed contentedly over his chest.

"I hoped you would come sooner than later," he said with a welcoming grin. Then, as she crossed the threshold of his home, he added, "You look stronger."

Iviana looked up at him as she took a seat inside. "What do you mean?"

"The first time you came to see me, you were like a frail bird. The last time, you were a lost sheep. This time...well, I suppose you're 'found.'"

"No animal parallel for the current me?"

"Mmm..." He thought a moment. "You're a lioness."

Iviana raised an eyebrow. "I'll accept that."

"Good. I wasn't the one who chose it."

Iviana was about to ask what he meant before she saw the mysterious white dove on his shoulder: the

15

one she had not seen since the last time she was with Marquen. Instead, she smiled at the word and commented, "I feel stronger, now that I think about it."

Marquen nodded. "Well...I get the feeling you came to see me for more than a friendly chat."

"I heard you came down from your mountain."

"Hill," he corrected with a smirk.

"So everyone insists." Iviana rolled her eyes. "Anyway...I was told you were with Rhimesh before she passed."

"I was," Marquen replied. He sat up and rested his elbows on the table to face her head on. "She asked for me that day—first person to do that in the fifteen years I've lived on this hill. She knew it was her time and wanted to relay a message before she was free to be with the Great One." He paused, looking straight into Iviana's eyes, but did not continue.

"Marquen, what was the message? And why haven't you told anyone? I think the realm deserves to know what her last words were."

"She wanted it to come from my lips to your ears."

Iviana sat up in her chair. "It's for me? What is it? Why did it need to come from you?"

"I suppose she wanted to be certain you would receive it."

"And you're the only person who can relay messages?"

"There are those who would share it with others—the council, namely—and then it may have been decided you should never learn what she wanted to tell you. I live on this hill and I speak to my own people rarely...let alone share secrets with them."

"Alright, I understand, but what did she say?"

"The Great One showed her something."

"She was a Seer? Funny, I never knew."

"No. She was a Translator. She could read or hear any language and understand it and when she spoke to someone who did not speak our language, they in turn understood her."

Iviana liked this idea. "Wow. Why haven't I heard of that one?"

"There are plenty who possess the gift, but it is not valued because there is rare occasion for its use. We all speak but one language in the Greater Archipelagos and, as you well know, we do not welcome many outsiders. At any rate, she is not a Seer."

"Yet, she saw something. What was it?"

"It was a parchment."

Iviana held her breath. "And...?"

"She said she could not read the words on the parchment because they glowed like the piercing rays of the sun. She claimed the Great One's voice spoke to her, saying, 'If the message of My heart's cry is not revealed, if not one can be found to fight on behalf of my people, I will be forgotten and they will be lost. Rhimesh, I need my warriors. Where are my warriors?' With that, her vision ceased. A few hours later, she relayed it to me. She made me promise I would tell you exactly what she had seen and been told."

Iviana sat back in her chair, her mind racing. "But why me? Why did she want *me* to know?"

Marquen looked straight into her bewildered eyes. "She needs you to seek that parchment. The message that must be known is inscribed on it and it is vital."

Iviana stood to her feet. "How in the world does she expect me to find some paper I've never seen before when I don't even know what's on it?"

"Well, glowing words should be fairly difficult to miss."

"Right. Have you ever seen the written word glow? Have you ever heard of such a thing until now? I wouldn't know where to begin."

"That's why she chose you. You're our only Seeker and your gift can lead you even when your physical mind lacks knowledge."

With these words, Iviana attempted to calm herself while Marquen studied her.

"I'm surprised," he commented.

"By what?"

"I'd have thought you would be sick of lazing around. I thought Seekers had fire in their blood— that they always had to be moving forward and seeking what lies ahead."

Iviana stood again. "Well, maybe I'm not a very good Seeker then," she offered and walked out of the cabin.

As Iviana made her way down the mountain, she regretted her reaction to his words. Nevertheless, she couldn't help feeling she was right. She couldn't just flip on her Seeker's fire when the need arose. At least, she didn't believe she could. It wasn't as if there were other Seekers to ask. She was the one and only. Her grandfather, Latos' son, had been the last of the Seekers before her.

By the time she had reached the dwelling area of the islanders and was passing the council hall, she had convinced herself of her correctness in the matter until the council meeting ended and Flynn happened upon her. Seeing she was upset by something, he eventually coaxed the explanation out of her, but his reaction was not what she had expected.

"We have to do it then," he said. "We have to honor Rhimesh, not to mention the Great One. I say we leave first thing tomorrow." With that, he stood to his feet as though about to make arrangements.

"What?" Iviana looked at him in surprise. "You can't go. You're the Realm Leader."

"Yes, and sometimes leaders help their Seekers do what they must. Besides, I could use a bit of adventure. Naii can take care of things while we're away. It shouldn't take long anyway. The last time you put your gift to use it took a good day or so to find what you sought."

Iviana didn't like this. If the Realm Leader accompanied her, the eyes of the whole planet would be on her quest. "You don't know it will be that simple again..."

"No, I don't," he admitted, "but I'm still going."

A smile slowly crept onto Iviana's face. "Alright," she forfeited. "Where do we go from here?"

"Before the council."

Iviana grimaced. "You know how much I hate that."

"Yes, but I'm Realm Leader now. It'll be different this time.

ॐ

Later that evening, Iviana rejoined Darist and Nimua and the three made their way to the Grand Pavilion for the evening banquet. As they walked, Iviana's stomach knotted itself into an aching mess. She knew well that word of her reappearance would have reached even beyond the Isle of Dragons by now, the way the islanders talked. The people led simple lives, so gossip in any form was the daily pastime. Anything having to do with the daring Seeker was the favored topic.

"Perhaps I should wait until tomorrow to attend," suggested Iviana when the pavilion was in sight. "My arrival will be old news by then."

"Oh, don't be such a chicken, Ivi," said Nimua. "It won't be like your first banquet, when you were an entirely new addition to the realm. Besides, it really doesn't matter *when* you show your face; you know they'll still whisper."

"Just ignore them," added Darist. "Make out like it doesn't bother you. As the only Seeker, you'll probably never be free of their attention. Just choose not to care and they'll eventually grow bored."

Iviana smiled. "Thanks, Darist. I'll try."

Once within, the staring certainly did occur as well as the gossip, but Iviana found it easier to ignore than expected. In truth, she reminded herself she did not care what they thought of her, so why should she care when they were at their rudest? It was at that time she must show them what they thought did not matter. Besides, there were fewer people who disapproved of her after she had found the next Realm Leader, so the number of those who stared at her was less than it would once have been.

"Iviana, the dragon-whisperer!" cried Brenna when she caught sight of her. "I had heard of your return, but couldn't seem to find you." She proceeded to embrace Iviana and pulled back with a large grin. "I'm so happy to see you again, friend."

Iviana was surprised by this show of affection for, though the two had previously been friends, they had not spent as much time together as she would have liked. Still, it was nice to know how much she meant to her. In truth, Iviana had missed Brenna as well. The brave nature-lover had always been perfectly kind and that was something Iviana appreciated.

Leilyn, too, followed Brenna's hug with one of her own and seemed to have missed Iviana almost as much, but Iviana struggled to imagine why. Though Leilyn had been less venomous once she'd engaged herself to Nico, she and Iviana had never formed a friendship. In fact, Iviana wondered if Leilyn was one of those people she might never be able to like. Just the same, she embraced Leilyn meaningfully, grateful the girl chose to be courteous.

Nico was the one to surprise her for, though he was yet engaged to Leilyn, his grudge against Iviana for not caring for him as he had for her had persisted. Iviana could live with this, however. It was better than his trying to win her affection. A wooing Nico had proved to be too much for her.

The hours of feasting continued without occurrence and Iviana was pleased she had attended. It was worth it to spend more time with the people she had missed so much and to see more of Brenna and even a little of Leilyn. And as Flynn understood she would not want attention brought on her, he did not make the announcement of her arrival as would have been correct and certainly as Rhimesh would have done.

To her friends, Iviana revealed Rhimesh's request that she seek the parchment and told them of her and Flynn's meeting with the council earlier that day, explaining how they had consented to the journey. In fact, their swift approval had surprised her more than she could convey, leaving her a little suspicious. She had attempted mentioning this to Flynn, but he had been too excited and would hear none of it.

At the news of her leaving the following day, Darist, Nimua and Brenna insisted they be allowed to go along and Iviana consented happily, though a sliver of nerves pricked at the back of her mind. Having her four friends along put a fair amount of responsibility on her shoulders, but, according to their insistence, this was something she would have to live with. Besides, she was certainly hesitant to leave them behind when she had only just been reunited with them.

After the banqueting festivities had concluded and Iviana bid her friends goodnight, she again made the hike up Seer's hill. Though being out after the banquet was frowned upon, she had ceased caring about the opinions of those who looked on her with judgment long ago. Besides, she was certain she would be unable to sleep until she patched things up with him.

This had not been a difficult task for, just as her friends had brushed off her having left them, Marquen simply wanted to know what her plans were now she had decided to fulfill Rhimesh's wishes. Iviana began with the meeting with the council, "Some were unconvinced the journey should be made considering Rhimesh wasn't known to be a Seer. But as she so recently passed, most of them were extremely hesitant to question it," Iviana told him.

"You say Flynn will go with you?" Marquen asked.

Iviana smirked, answering, "Yes. Once they had come to the decision I should go, that was the next matter to be discussed; it turns out Flynn has a way with words when he really wants something…"

Marquen smiled his understanding. "Who will take his place as Realm Leader while he is away?"

"Naii. She is one of the very few who can be trusted not only to make solid decisions and give wise council, but to step down once he returns."

"Mm." Marquen seemed unusually distracted. "That's true."

"What's on your mind?"

"I would like to go with you."

He certainly had her attention with that

statement. "*Really?*"

"I feel that, since I was the one with whom Rhimesh shared her vision, I might be of use in your search."

"But I thought you never left your hill?"

"Yes," he replied with a sigh. A smile slowly crept onto his face. "Doesn't that sound like it would grow boring after a while?"

Iviana raised her brows. "I suppose. But I thought you were this self-sufficient being who didn't need anyone but the Great One."

"Oh, that's true. He is the finest company one could ask for, but I think He's ready for me to step down from my mountain and have an adventure."

"'Mountain', huh?" Iviana stood to her feet, ready to depart. "That's what I thought."

‷2‶

IVIANA WATCHED THE Isle of Dragons diminish in the wild rush of flight. Perched upon Tragor's ascending frame, she breathed a deeply contented sigh. In all her previous travels, she had never had so many companions by her side and she could not help being grateful they had come. For the first time since learning of Rhimesh's wishes, she felt anticipation for the journey ahead.

Seated upon a creamy-white dragon, Flynn released a hardy laugh. It seemed Brenna, seated behind him, had made some joke about Nimua and Marquen, who rode together just beyond. The latter were in profound discussion as usual and Iviana was glad they had ridden together. Darist's dragon currently flying on the right side of Iviana and Tragor. He had been forced to ride alone since Tragor had proven he would have no more to do with Darist than he would anyone else. Still, he looked as if he was enjoying himself as he bent to whisper something to his powerful dragon after flashing a grin Iviana's way.

Iviana dwelled on how thoughtful Darist had been in taking care of her hut while she was away, even though there was no way he could have been certain she would ever return. After all, a friend who left without so much as a goodbye might never be expected to do the right thing in returning. Still, as far as she knew, all her friends had trusted she would not abandon their friendship forever.

She shook herself, for there were more important things to be worrying about—such as exactly *where* they were going. Her Seeker's gift was supposed to be leading them, but she did not feel the fire as she should—not yet, anyway. Without it, she was utterly lost. Thus far, Tragor was taking the lead while she waited for guidance, but she would need to choose a direction soon. Flying aimlessly with all this company wasn't an option. The others assumed she knew where she was going and that made her nervous—so nervous she was almost regretting allowing them to join her.

Iviana patted Tragor's neck. "I don't suppose *you* know where to go?"

He ignored her.

"Thanks," she muttered.

What about You, Great One? Can't You *help? Are You listening?*

There was no reply.

"Great."

There was a good chance this journey would end a fruitless one, but it could not be avoided. It had been the plea of the Great One spoken from the lips of a dying woman and one whom Iviana had respected. Everything would be perfectly fine so long as her gift began working soon.

∽

Hours later, the sun was setting and Iviana knew they must find a place to rest for the evening. This was a difficult task, however, on a planet made up of numerous islands and archipelagos—some closer together than others. But before long, Tragor led them to a single island that appeared to be the only land for miles. It didn't look to be populated, which meant they would have no roof over their heads nor beds beneath them, but it was better than trying to sleep on the back of a dragon. Moreover, the island flourished beautifully with colorful plant-life and the view of its towering mountains was spectacular.

"Are there really islands yet to be discovered?" Iviana asked while they set up camp. Nimua had just commented she believed the island was uncharted.

"Oh, yes," Nimua replied. "It's hard to believe, but it's a big world and it's difficult to discover where every piece of land is when you can't walk from one section to another like on Kaern. Explorers spend much of their lives searching for undiscovered islands, but there aren't as many explorers as one would think. Who knows how long it will be before we've truly mapped the planet?

"Now, a *really* intriguing mystery is the island that disappeared some time ago...or so I've heard. There are many who claim it isn't true, but for those whose ancestors vanished with it, it's no myth."

"I suppose not," Iviana replied through a yawn. It had been a stressful day and she was in dire need of rest.

"I personally don't believe it," added Darist. "It's not possible for an island to disappear."

"Then what explanation would you give?" asked Brenna.

Darist thought a while, then shrugged. "I couldn't say. But there must be one."

Flynn rubbed his chin. "I haven't heard of this. I will have to look into it when we return. It is certainly an intriguing thought. Why has there been no ongoing investigation?"

Nimua shrugged. "It was nearly a hundred years ago, if I'm correct. I suppose everyone just moved on."

"Well, perhaps that will be our next venture," put in Marquen.

Iviana looked at him in her surprise. That Marquen had come on this journey was intriguing enough. She hadn't realized he planned to continue his new life among them afterward—a fact she would not at all mind. Marquen meant a lot to her, for he always seemed to have an answer when she needed one. Just having him with them now was reassuring. She felt he was a support to be well appreciated and it made her feel less alone. He knew the Great One well. If Iviana could not get them where they needed to be, perhaps he could.

It wasn't long before the group finished their meal. It was a miracle no one had asked what direction they would take in the morning, though Marquen had sent her a few knowing looks. It was often helpful he seemed all-knowing, but she was beginning to find there could be a small downside.

She was just grateful he had the tact to keep it to himself.

At least he *won't be surprised if it turns out my gift isn't working.*

Iviana spared no time in tucking herself into the little makeshift bed the young women had made in their tent. Nimua was a big believer in the comfort of pillows and had piled the ground with them. Tucking her face against a large fluffy one, Iviana forced herself to release her anxiety over what she would do the following day if her gift did not guide her. Allowing her drooping lids to flutter closed, she fell into a deep, much needed slumber.

∾

There was no way of knowing the time when a great clap of thunder caused the ground beneath them to tremble, forcibly waking them from their much needed sleep. The menacing thunder was soon followed by a great gust of wind that attempted to rip the young women's' tent from over them. As they attempted to repack their things, Darist rushed in, shouting for them to take the tent down before it was captured by the storm.

When the girls hurried out, they were immediately saturated as the fearsome wind made needles of the rain and pushed and pulled them about at its volition. As the ocean began to heave itself over the beach and toward the camp, Darist raced over and bundled their tent up in his arms.

"Where do we go?" Iviana called.

He ran inland, shouting back, "Marquen says there's a cave further in." As there was no sign of Flynn or Marquen, Iviana assumed they were already on their way with their tent and belongings.

Soon, the expected cave was in view, but it occurred to Iviana she had no idea where Tragor and the other dragons were. She frantically looked about, but there was no sign of them.

Taking Brenna by the shoulder, she relayed she was going to look for Tragor. Poor Brenna tried desperately to stop her, but Iviana had to be certain Tragor was alright. Though he was a mighty dragon, he had needed her help before. He just might need her again. The wind pressed fiercely against her, succeeding in knocking her off her feet numerous times and thunder resounded like a looming giant in her wake, but Iviana kept on, determined as a mad woman.

This is some beginning, she thought bitterly.

But Iviana realized she had not yet seen the heart of this storm when, upon reaching the beach, a seething, brooding wave raised itself heavenward, preparing to crash over all below and crush Iviana under its might. She froze as lightning struck the ground only a few feet away. It was as if this storm was attempting to heap itself on her like a weeping army of rage and she was only one of the helpless granules of smoking sand under the hot strike of lightning at the center of its mighty symphony.

Suddenly, she was snatched up into the talons of a dragon and carried clumsily over the crashing swell. It sprayed spitefully after the fleeing duo who knew they had only just escaped their end. Iviana recognized Tragor as he struggled through the storm. Twice, he nearly dropped her before finally plummeting to the ground a few yards from the cave. The two were unharmed, but Tragor refused to remain, knowing he was too large for the refuge. He penetrated her eyes with his, conveying he would be alright. With that, he left her. Iviana shouted after him, but Darist appeared at her side, took hold of her arm and drug her toward the cave.

They were still some yards from the shelter when a twisting funnel of cloud appeared overhead. Iviana panicked, feeling its pull as the trees and foliage around them began to quiver and lift from the ground. Working quickly, Darist flung Iviana over his shoulder and ran toward the cave with every bit of anointed strength the Great One had given him. Still, it seemed as though the funnel would take them until Iviana shrieked the first words that came to her, *"Great One, please!"*

From over Darist's shoulder, Iviana watched in disbelief as the funnel disappeared just as they entered the safety of the cavern.

Darist carefully placed Iviana upon the rocky floor of the cave, looking her over as if making certain she was in one piece.

"Thank you, Darist," she whispered between exhausted breaths.

Nimua rushed over and took them up in her arms. "I thought you two were goners!"

Flynn patted Darist on the back before kneeling beside Iviana. "That was pretty stupid, you know," he said more seriously than she had ever heard him speak. He squeezed her hand and returned to organizing the mess of their possessions.

"Not so fast, Flynn," Nimua called after him. "Aren't you going to tell them what happened?"

Flynn shrugged and lifted a section of torn tent.

Iviana looked to Flynn, then back to Nimua.

35

"Well...what happened?"

"He made the funnel cloud vanish," Nimua explained, not without some awe.

Iviana and Darist looked doubtful.

"Don't look at me like I'm crazy! He *did.* He just shouted, 'Be gone!' and so it was."

Iviana peered back at Flynn, who appeared uncomfortable.

"I don't know how to explain it," he said quietly. "It was as if the Great One took possession of me and caused the words to be said."

Marquen nodded. "I felt Him here."

Iviana watched Flynn as he worked. He appeared nervous and Iviana knew the power of his words over the forming tornado had startled him. In truth, it surprised her as well. Who could know what he was capable of when his gift had never been seen? They would certainly have to explore the possibilities when they had completed their journey.

⳹

A while later, the storm settled and the group warmed themselves around a small fire inside the cave. Marquen sat jotting in a journal and Nimua and Darist were chatting about the events of the evening. Iviana absently listened, but was too weary to relive it with them. Besides, she hadn't seen the two get on so well since she'd rejoined them and wanted to leave them be. She liked them as a couple, but they certainly hadn't acted like one recently and Nimua refused to talk about it.

At the sound of their laughter, Iviana noticed for the first time how close Flynn and Brenna had grown. She couldn't say when this had begun, as she had been away, but she wondered if the two would make a match as well. Observing them closely, she could see what Flynn saw in Brenna. She had always been kind and gracious and this hadn't changed. If anything, she was even sweeter and tactfully shared her opinions. Iviana was certain Flynn, at least, had feelings for her, but wondered how Brenna felt.

There was one thing that bothered her, however. She knew that in the moment one becomes Realm Leader of the Greater Archipelagos, their aging process is supposed to have halted. What did that mean for the person they wanted to spend their life with? Was the leader expected to watch their spouse grow old while they were forced into agelessness until, at some point, death finds them? The idea of the agelessness was a little unnatural to Iviana. She couldn't imagine living possibly hundreds of years, serving an entire realm as leader; it sounded exhausting. Doing it alone seemed unthinkable.

Iviana cast her eye on Marquen and started in his direction.

"Ah, the Seeker comes this way," he murmured over his writing.

Iviana sat beside him. "Your dove tell you that?"

"My peripheral vision is keen. I've been absently watching you, wondering what could have put that wrinkle of consternation between your brows."

"I've been wondering about the agelessness of the Realm Leader."

"What about it?"

"Well...what happens if they decide to marry?"

Marquen smirked. "You hoping to wed our leader?"

Iviana blushed. She hadn't realized it would sound like she wanted him for herself. He was *Flynn*...not *her* Flynn. "Of course not."

Marquen looked up from his writing. "Don't fret, oh, Seeker. I was only teasing."

"Oh."

"You're wondering what it would be like for the spouse of a Realm Leader to grow old and die while the other remained just as sturdy and young looking as ever."

"Exactly."

"There is a simple fix if one chooses to enter into the complexity of the situation." He paused a moment to jot something down in his journal.

"Well, go on," Iviana urged impatiently.

He continued as he wrote. "Have you ever heard the phrase 'the two shall become one?'"

Iviana nodded.

"Should one find they are willing to enter into a lifetime without the natural aging process, they may easily do so. It is as simple as the two stating their wedding vows under the anointing of the Great One. The moment a certain phrase is said along the lines of their being joined as one, they share the responsibilities as Realm Leader, including the agelessness. However, should the official Realm Leader pass away, the other begins to age a little more rapidly than is perfectly natural, if they have not passed away already."

"That's a lot to ask of someone, though, isn't it?"

Marquen nodded. "Why do you think Rhimesh never married? I believe your great-grandfather was only the second Realm Leader in our history to have entered into matrimony. Which, after the complexity of his situation, may have been another reason Rhimesh never married."

Iviana sat quietly, letting that sink in. She almost felt guilty for having pulled Flynn into his current position. It was no secret the authority his job entailed frightened him, for he had said as much when she had first arrived. Still, there was nothing she could do now.

Glancing at Marquen's swift pen, she remarked, "So, you write?"

"What do you think I do all day in the mountains?"

"*Hills...*" she corrected with a grin. "I don't know. I've always wondered."

"Well, I write."

"About what?"

"What the Great One shows me. What I see from my *hill.* I also write about you."

Iviana blinked at him. "*Me?*"

"Yes."

"Why?"

He continued writing as he said, "Because there's something about you, Ivi. You don't make sense. Nobody just runs into a dragon and then shows up in the Greater Archipelagos from another *universe* with no foreknowledge of us. Your whole life is a big question, Iviana. It's as if you were kept in waiting, hidden from our worlds, and then you were suddenly...released...into something." He looked up at her. "I don't know what it is yet, but the Great One is excited about you." He smiled. "He's *so* excited about you. His heart beats faster when He thinks about you...in anticipation."

Iviana gulped. "Anticipation of what?"

He looked deep into her eyes, searching. "I don't know," he said. "But I want to be there when it happens."

He returned to his writing and Iviana fell silent. She would never have guessed Marquen was thinking all of *that* about her. It was amazing he kept such thoughts inside him all the time, always up on his hill, without any human interaction but what Nimua offered from time to time, the whole island looking on him in disapproval. What stories could he tell about his time in the hills? What had really caused him to abandon his solitude and accompany her on this journey?

"You should probably try to catch a few more hours shut-eye before we continue our journey tomorrow.

Iviana nodded. Already, she was struggling to keep awake, but the others' wakefulness had dissuaded her from attempting slumber...not to mention the excitement of the storm she and Darist had only just survived.

"The others will quiet down when they see you tuck into your bed."

Iviana smiled as she rose to gather one of the now dry, if slightly damp, blankets from beside the fire and a dry shirt to roll up as a pillow. She knew Marquen was correct. Her friends were considerate that way. She was glad no one like Leilyn had joined them to detract from the camaraderie of the group. It was certainly something to be cherished.

∞ 3 ∞

HAVING AWOKEN BEFORE the others, Iviana sleepily wandered onto the beach in hopes of finding Tragor. What she found instead was rather more intriguing, if not satisfying. It was her great-grandfather and former Realm Leader of the Greater Archipelagos, Latos, or, rather, his likeness. Carved out of a large piece of silver rock was a man who, at first sight, looked strikingly similar to Iviana. However, the likeness was male with surprisingly lively eyes for a statue. Those eyes seemed to gaze directly into hers and, for whatever reason, nearly drew her to tears.

Iviana discovered words etched at the base of the figure and knelt to study them. They were written in an unfamiliar language, but she was astonished to find she understood their meaning.

Latos: Beloved Friend of the Great Being, it read.

Iviana assumed it was a monument created by someone who had discovered the island before her and her friends, though she could in no way be certain when it was made. It was beautiful work. Iviana felt if she spoke to him, he might reply, it was so realistic. His eyes and smile drew her in, almost capturing her confidence. She thought if it truly were he before her, she would follow him anywhere, attempting to learn what made him smile so and gave him such assurance.

It's hard to believe this man's life could have been taken by Aradia, yet mine was not, she thought, tracing his shoulder-length hair with her fingers.

Abruptly, she glanced back to his eyes and found they were no longer gazing directly at her but toward the water she was standing in. For, to view the statue, one had to walk along the shallow waters surrounding the cliff-face on this side of the island. Iviana felt if he were alive he would be trying to tell her something. Even his smile did not appear so full of joy anymore, but was almost frustrated in trying to convey something. Iviana blinked and all that she thought she had seen on his face was no more.

Still, she turned around to face the bulk of the ocean behind her. Slowly, she walked further out until the water reached her knees, then her waist and then shoulders. Taking a deep breath, she tucked her head beneath the water.

All was blurry as her eyes adjusted. She swam in the warm, soothing water searching for what, she did not know, until a creature that looked something like a dragon appeared in the distance. Iviana's heart beat faster and she wondered if Latos had been signaling a warning, if anything at all. She knew she had no reason to fear if this creature was a dragon, but dragons, she knew, could not swim.

Working against the fear in her stomach, Iviana swam to the surface, stole another breath and dove further in. She was struck by how calm the ocean was this morning when the dragon-like creature appeared again, followed by yet another. They moved with as much grace as a dragon above water, although it was magnified beneath it. Indeed, as she drew closer, Iviana questioned if the creatures were dragons after all.

Again, she drew nearer, despite the rate at which her heart beat, until a large shadow moved overhead. Iviana froze beneath the blue substance, struck with sudden terror. Much like when the lightning had struck beside her the night before, she could not move and her lungs were beginning to plead for air. Childishly, Iviana squeezed her eyes closed, as if the swimming serpent to whom the shadow belonged would flee her. Even so, she desperately needed air. Opening her eyes a crack, she gasped, nearly choking. Swimming in the space before her was a creature she knew very well, even by name: Tragor, the Great Dragon of the Ages.

The dragon looked almost pleased to see her. If dragons could smile, she thought surely he was. He moved nearer, offering his face to be pet. He then tossed his head behind him, as if signaling she should follow, but Iviana needed oxygen. She swiftly swam to the surface, heaved a few breaths and then the largest she could manage and returned to Tragor.

She had only to take hold of his neck as he pulled her wherever he wished. As her dragon-friend swam with intent, Iviana grew curious. What could he wish to show her? It was surprise enough he could swim—that apparently all dragons could, for others appeared around them—but what other enigmas lay within the sea? As the dragon swam deeper, Iviana was thankful it was her trusted friend that brought her all this way, else she would certainly panic.

She knew she would have to make Tragor take her to the surface again just as a curious shape on the bottom of the ocean floor came into view. Squinting into the distance in an attempt to make it out, she made ready to motion that she needed air, but she nearly lost her grip on his neck when his speed changed and they were accelerating forward.

Soon, a shimmering, semi-transparent dome on the sandy surface of the ocean floor was not far ahead. Tragor continued gaining speed as they drew nearer and Iviana realized the lack of oxygen was playing tricks, for within the dome appeared a colorful city, busy with people and unusual, towering structures.

Iviana feared she was near fainting and wanted to pull up to the surface, but Tragor was moving too swiftly for her to do anything but hold on. It occurred to her they were going to crash into the dome when her dragon did the very thing she feared. But no collision took place. Instead, there was a stretching or shoving of whatever substance the shimmering dome was made of until they passed through and were soaring over the colorful city below.

And Iviana could *breathe.*

She was faint and rested on Tragor's back, feeding her screaming lungs all the oxygen they would take. Gracefully, Tragor flew over the impossible city, drawing nearer the ground with a purpose. Despite the fact that the sun's rays could not possibly reach so far beneath the water, it was beautifully lighted within the dome. Iviana attempted to lift her head in search of some light source, but could discover none.

When Tragor finally landed, Iviana realized she had closed her weary eyes. Curiously, they fluttered open to reveal a large corridor—large enough even for Tragor to fit—with long stretches of rounded metal tubes going every which way above them. Tragor attempted to nudge her off, so she shakily slid off his back and collapsed on the floor.

༄

Iviana became conscious of someone poking her arm. She was a little relieved to find all that had taken place was only a dream, but disappointed she still had no idea of Tragor's well-being. There was something amiss, however, for the murmuring over her groggy head did not sound like her traveling companions.

Had she never left the Isle of Dragons and the whole of their travels been a dream? If so, who could possibly be in her bedroom? She did not recall having gone to bed. In fact, she did not feel as though she was in her cozy bed at all, but on some wholly uncomfortable surface.

Struck with the thought that her underwater journey with Tragor into a city that dwelt beneath the sea had not been a fanciful dream after all, Iviana opened her eyes.

"We have been waiting for you, Glory-Bringer," the voice of an aged man spoke over her.

Iviana sat up quickly and peered at the people that crouched and stood around her. She did not recognize one of them.

"Then you must have the wrong person," she replied.

"No, they do not," said a familiar voice.

Iviana could not discover from whom the words escaped until a beautiful woman in Kierelian garb stepped forward. Slowly, Iviana attached the woman's voice and face with a vague memory. She recalled the visit she had taken to the Isle of Knowledge some time ago—the first time she had come to the Greater Archipelagos. The Isle of Knowledge had been the first island she visited after the Isle of Dragons. While there, she had met a beautiful woman in a Kierelian cape. The woman had known who she was and conveyed she knew more, but would not say it. Yet, she promised she would meet with Iviana again in the future. Iviana supposed that future was now.

"Chamaeleo?" Iviana recalled the woman's name from the recesses of her memory. "Where am I?"

"The lost Isle of Atlantyss," Chamaeleo replied. "Though I don't suppose you'll have heard much of us since you've been spending most of your time on Kaern.

Iviana shook her head. "No. Should I have?"

"Not at all," she replied laughingly. "It would be most worrisome if you had, in any case. This city has been concealed for over a hundred years. Its whereabouts should be completely unknown to those in the Greater Archipelagos, let alone in your home world."

"Is it not your home world as well?"

"What makes you ask that?"

"Your clothing."

Chamaeleo peered down at herself. "Of course. Well, I suppose you could call it my home. I have spent much time there."

When a man with graying beard and partially bald head cleared his throat, Iviana became aware of those around her again and felt a little self-conscious.

The bearded man followed his throat-clearing with, "We welcome you most heartily, Iviana of Kierelia."

Chamaeleo smiled and explained, "This is Kais Teodores, though most call him Kais Teo."

Iviana nodded and smiled at the man. She was about to hold her arm out to shake his from where she sat when a young man and woman, who looked to be near her own age, helped her to her feet.

"And these two are Junior Kais Merrick and Aedis." Chamaeleo gestured to the young man who had a piece of clear glass over each eye connected by a wire that wrapped over his ears, then to the young woman with deep red hair who offered her a quick nod and smile.

Chamaeleo continued to introduce Iviana to the men and women of various ages around her. In all, there were about seven surrounding, including Chamaeleo, and most had the Kais or Junior Kais before their name. Considering this, Iviana understood it to be a sort of title such as "sir" in her world.

The last of these, a largely built man with very dark skin by the name of Kais Tybalt, knelt before her. Taking her hand in his and leaning his forehead against it, he said, "I am honored to have lived while you are in this world. I am honored, further, to have laid eyes on you in my lifetime and, still further, to have made your acquaintance." He raised his head and gazed on her face. "I wish you the Great One's guidance and protection in all that is to come."

Iviana was shocked by the man's behavior toward her and wished to assure him he was mistaken in his speech, but the smiling Chamaeleo nodded, conveying he was not. Iviana's mouth fell open a little. All she could do was look into the face of the man who knelt before her and nod. This satisfied him greatly and he returned to where he had previously stood.

"I am certain we have done nothing but confuse you from the moment you arrived," said Kais Teo of the balding head. "Even as we have faithfully anticipated your arrival for some time, we seem to have been caught ill prepared for it."

Iviana knew he wanted to ease her, but he only succeeded in confusing her further. Could it be true these people had been waiting for *her*? Why? What could have given them cause to hope for her arrival?

With these questions and more circling within, she turned to Chamaeleo.

The beautiful woman understood. "Come. Let us speak in private, Iviana."

Iviana agreed and followed her into a small adjoining room.

As Iviana took a seat beside a unique looking contraption she was told was used to provide warmth, Chamaeleo began with, "Will you explain how you have come to be in our city at this time? Obviously, we saw you with the Great Dragon of the Ages. He and his other companions gave us a fright when they took shelter here during the storm last night. That was before we knew they were with you, of course. We know by sight most of the dragons that usually venture in, you see. But tell me, how have you come to discover us?"

"It's a little hard to explain without starting at the beginning."

"Then do so freely. I am all ears."

Iviana shifted in her seat. "Well, it began in my home within the Kierelian kingdom of Kaern. I felt the Realm Leader, Rhimesh, had passed on."

Chamaeleo nodded. "As did I."

Iviana looked her over a moment. Despite her Kierelian garb, this meant Chamaeleo had the blood of those who lived in the Greater Archipelagos. She had been wondering, previously, if she was perhaps not of the Greater Archipelagos and had stumbled in somehow, as she had. The woman was just so different from everyone she had met in the realm.

"Tragor came for me and brought me back to the Greater Archipelagos."

"If I may interrupt you," Chamaeleo began, "I'm curious. Had the woman's death not occurred, would you ever have returned?"

Iviana looked within. She had been avoiding that question the entirety of her time away. "I don't believe so," she finally admitted.

The woman smiled knowingly in response, but that was all.

Iviana continued, "Upon my return, I was told Rhimesh had left a message for me at the time of her death. She asked that I seek a parchment containing information the Great One desires the Greater Archipelagos to know."

"And she wanted you to use your Seeker's gift."

"Yes."

"What troubles you, Iviana?" Chamaeleo asked pensively.

Iviana felt both caught and a little relieved at once. "I have not felt the Seeker's fire for some time.

We camped on the island nearby only because we needed to rest for the evening. The others believe I know what I'm doing, but truly, I feel clueless."

Chamaeleo was thoughtful and seemed to be listening for something before she said, "My reply to your anxiety is this: how did you find Atlantyss?"

Iviana was confused. "I believe it was that dreadful storm last night; I was nearly swept up in it. At any rate, I can only suppose Tragor was thrust into the water near Atlantyss and found you. I found the statue of Latos on the beach this morning and felt...I don't know...that I ought to go for a swim. That's when Tragor found me and brought me here."

Chamaeleo looked her over, almost as if she was waiting for Iviana to realize something, but Iviana couldn't put her finger on what.

"Chamaeleo?" she urged.

"The Great One is a creative Being. His ways are often inexplicable, but altogether clever when it comes right down to it. Situations we consider out of the ordinary or frightening, He views as...mmm...*attention-grabbing*." She wore an almost ornery grin as she spoke the last.

"Chamaeleo," Iviana began, "though, in truth, I feel the opposite, you are a stranger to me. I cannot read into whatever it is you're trying to convey."

The woman looked her over again and then laughed—not a mocking laugh, but a perfectly congenial one that sounded something like the chiming of bells. Iviana nearly laughed with her, though she had no idea what was so comical.

"Oh, Iviana, don't be so closed-minded. I believe everything you have told me is the obvious answer to your cares. You have been made aware of the precious gift He has bestowed upon you, but that does not mean that is the tool He will use in order to lead you through the journey He has prepared for you. His ways are generally beyond us. Can you not see that your finding this island was no accident? No one else has found it in all the time it has been below this honeyed ocean. How came you to choose the very island nearby? A terrifying storm threatens your 'randomly' selected island resulting in *your* dragon finding us. You happen to find the monument of Latos and, for whatever reason, you made your way below the waves to find the one who could bring you to us. As I said, the Great One works in mysteriously clever ways."

"So...you're saying the Great One led me here on purpose...without using my gift? Why?"

"Oh, who knows why? He has His secrets. It is our job to know they are born of goodness—that He works for more than one purpose."

"What are His purposes?"

"Perhaps the people here needed hope, so He brought you here only that they might see your face. Perhaps it is important you know we are here, to support you if for no greater purpose. I cannot say for certain."

Iviana looked up at her. "Well, where am I to go from here?"

The lady smiled, her big brown eyes shining brightly. "That is not for me to know. Even so, you have seen the faith the people of Atlantyss have in you and learned there are prophecies foreshadowing your future. You can be certain, if you place your trust in the Great One, your destiny will come to pass. And it is a great future, even if it is not what you would have dreamed for yourself."

"Can you tell me now the things you could not tell me when we first met?"

"Of course not and I would prefer you not ask the others anything about the things that have been prophesied either. I think it will be much more fun that way. Indeed, I think if you do ask, you might be a little frightened."

"Well, that comment is a little frightening," Iviana replied with a wry grin.

Chamaeleo laughed the perfectly congenial laugh again. "I will tell you this: your coming to the Greater Archipelagos has been known by the people of this city since before it was placed beneath the ocean. Many have been informed of the grand things in store for you and…oh, my dear, I'm sorry. I really cannot say more or I will spoil it."

Iviana shrugged, dearly wishing to know more, but it was not in her nature to beg a secret. "Very well," she said instead. "Can you explain this beautiful city to me then? It's like nothing I could have ever dreamed."

"That is certainly feasible, but I'm afraid I've got somewhere to be now and this will be the last time I see you within this city for the time being. I will have Merrick and Aedis give you a tour and find you a comfortable place to stay for the night."

"Oh, no, I can't stay. I have friends waiting for me above."

"*Above?*" Chamaeleo's tone changed entirely. "You don't mean they're on that forsaken island with the statue of Latos on it, do you?"

"Well...yes." Iviana was troubled by the worry on Chamaeleo's face.

"You should know the people here rather avoid that island at all costs. I cannot say precisely why, but I gather there have been some strange occurrences in past and it has been deemed unsafe..." Chamaeleo took a breath and continued, "Still, I did not mean to worry you and I am certain your friends are alright. However, as soon as you return, be sure to move on from it. I'm not saying the things I've heard are anything but foolish tales...but you never know."

"Thank you for the warning," Iviana replied graciously, though she thought Chamaeleo's last remark was probably more accurate. "It seemed perfectly safe last night...well, before the storm. We will move on, however."

"I won't have you leave without a tour, though. You simply must see a little of this city."

"Thank you, Chamaeleo. I'm so glad I met you again. You have restored me a little with your wisdom."

Chamaeleo smiled. "I wish you luck in your current journey. I have a feeling it will be...*intriguing.*"

Chamaeleo opened the door and motioned to young Merrick and Aedis who were not far, though the others had gone. "I would like the two of you to show Iviana around and then arrange for her to travel back to the surface. She has friends waiting for her and a mission to complete." She raised a playful brow and said, "I trust the two of you will not overwhelm her with the intense deference some of our older citizens have conveyed."

"Of course, Chamaeleo," Aedis replied matter-of-factly. Merrick didn't appear quite as certain, revealed by a glimmer of excitement in his eyes, but eagerly nodded his agreement.

❧4❧

AEDIS AND MERRICK led Iviana through a long echoing corridor. Everything thus far was far more foreign than when she had first seen the Isle of Dragons. The buildings on that island were small and simple, whereas this one was very large with numerous rooms and hallways; its architecture was like nothing she had ever seen. It had long square and circular tubes that ran down the ceiling with walls that were made of material she was not familiar with. On these were hung placards that read warnings, reminders and inspirational messages. The color scheme throughout was of various shades of blue and gray, a contrast to the colorful city she had seen when passing through the dome.

"We're very happy to make your acquaintance," the red-headed Aedis said, reaching out her hand. Iviana took it and gave it a shake.

"Yes, very honored," young Merrick mumbled bashfully.

Aedis rolled her eyes confidingly. "He's a little awestruck," she whispered.

"I see," Iviana replied. Wishing to change the subject, she added, "Tell me, why this scheme of colors?"

"You mean it's plainer than the rest of the city? This is the creative engineering building and this wing is meant to be a place where the Kais can work without distraction. There are other wings—also connected with the Kais' work—that are far more inspiring. However, we won't have time to visit those today. There are more interesting things to be seen."

"The Kais. What sort of title is that?"

The Kais are a select group of Inventors as well as the exceptionally creative and ingenious. All are tested at the end of schooling and those who suit what they're looking for are taken on as 'Junior Kais' before potentially joining the Kais' team. Just now, Merrick and I are the only Junior Kais on staff. It's a very selective program and rather an honor at that."

"Oh, yes, very honored..." Merrick commented quietly.

Aedis smiled. "Merrick is a mathematical

genius...and an introvert."

"I see. You say 'schooling' and 'mathematical'..."

"Oh, yes. The Greater Archipelagos has no schooling, have they? It means learning. We attend a series of lectures daily from age eight until around the age of sixteen to twenty depending on the student. As for 'mathematical'...that would take some time."

"I wish I could have attended such lectures. Although, I did grow up in a sort of learning environment working with my mentor."

"Your mentor?"

"She was a Healer and taught me everything she knew."

"Then you're a Healer. I think that is one of the most precious gifts. I, myself, am an Inventor. Oh, just follow Merrick through that door."

With a gasp, Iviana stepped out into the underwater city. She had somehow forgotten they were truly under the ocean, protected by some magical dome. Looking about, there was no denying her fascination with Atlantyss. The little world around her was beyond anything she had ever seen or dreamed. It made her believe anything was possible with the Great One. He surely must be masterful if His gifted ones had created a place such as this. Iviana thought if the whole of the Greater

Archipelagos used their gifts in this manner, it would be an entirely different place.

The path they traveled was not made of dirt or sand, but of a solid rock-like mass that had been placed by the people of the city. Iviana enjoyed its smoothness beneath her feet. If this sort of thing were discovered by the outside world, she thought it would certainly be placed over every road and footpath.

Peering toward the top of the dome, Iviana found there were not only dragons soaring about but small flying contraptions that transported a single person at a time to different places throughout the city. Aedis called these "nelepyres," named for the man who invented them. It was all Iviana could do to keep from begging to be taken for a ride.

Some of the structures soared almost to the very top of the dome, while others were not quite as tall, but still far taller than any the Greater Archipelagos could boast. Every building was unique in color, shape and size and created a vibrant setting for everyday life. There were some buildings very similar to the homes on the Isle of Dragons. These appeared much older than the other buildings. Aedis explained these newer structures had been built only during the last hundred years that the island had been within the ocean.

"In fact, there is an architecture wing in the Kais buildings. The Kais who work there have been renovating the city for the entirety of our seclusion," Aedis explained.

"But where does the light come from?" Iviana questioned.

Aedis shrugged. "We don't know exactly how it works. You see, the dome seems to shine its own light over the city. It works similar to the sun in that it helps things grow, it darkens our skin, but, of course, it's quite different from the sun. To be perfectly honest, the dome and its light are one of those things the Great One has supplied that we may never understand."

"What about night?"

"It fades when the sun does," Merrick answered quickly. He smiled then, as if pleased he had finally been able to use coherent words.

"Fascinating," Iviana replied. "How is all of this possible? How were any of these things thought up at all?" She gestured to the nelepyres, the buildings, the roads.

"The Inventors," Aedis supplied.

Iviana nodded. "You've mentioned them several times...It is a gift?"

"Yes. I didn't realize you hadn't heard of them. They create and build things and, well, the word is 'invent.'" Aedis thought a moment, searching for a good example. "Do you know of the door in Jaela's Cavern—the one that leads into Kierelia?"

"Yes."

"Did you cross that barrier?"

"No. It wouldn't open for me."

"Well, that door is probably the only thing the Inventors above really have to show for their skill. You see, the portal didn't always have a door; the door was added by Inventors. It was designed to recognize those who live in the Greater Archipelagos, those who share our blood but have not set foot here previously and those who do not fall under either category. The first of these it allows to pass through, relays a message to the next and simply stands steadfast against the last. Now, you see, knowing that such a thing was created, our city isn't so surprising. While those outside our city have been smothered under the law of the council and been made only to use their gift when the council decides they have need of it, we have been hidden away and flourished in our freedom. Many of us believe the reason we were concealed was so, when the time comes, we may rise to the surface and share our knowledge, inventions and ideals with a people who will receive them."

"Only allowed to use it when the council says so? That's *ridiculous*. Why were they ever allowed to build that door at all, then? What's the use?"

"They needed to use the skill of the Inventors so not just anyone could walk through that portal. Though I believe the Great One meant it to be a free entrance for any who discover it, somewhere along the line our people decided that was inconvenient. In a few words, despite their anxiety over the Inventor's gift, it was deemed necessary to allow them to use it. But, until they deem another project worthy, the Inventors above are restrained."

Suddenly, a middle-aged woman interrupted their tour and pulled Merrick aside. Iviana could not hear what was said, but noticed the woman glance at her a few times with expressions of both wonder and anxiety. When the two finished their conversation, Merrick returned to the young women with some anxiety.

"There is something I have been told to ask you," he admitted.

"What is it Merrick? Do go on," Iviana kindly urged.

"We understand the Realm Leader is above,

waiting for you."

"Yes, he is."

"I'm supposed to ask that you not tell him or anyone else about us."

Iviana pondered this a moment. "I suppose it would be dangerous for you, wouldn't it? And it would put Flynn in a difficult position..."

"Yes," Aedis agreed. "Imagine the Greater Archipelagos, in its current frame of mind, discovering what we have become. We must not be discovered until the Great One sees fit to raise us again."

Iviana nodded, though she couldn't begin to understand what she meant by "until the Great One sees fit to raise us." Iviana had assumed they had somehow created the dome themselves and found some way to sink the island...but then, of course, they would have been able to explain the way the light worked and Aedis had made it clear that was a mystery to them. So, how *had* they come to be here and for what purpose?

Iviana realized Aedis and Merrick were looking at her anxiously and remembered they were awaiting an answer. "Er...well, it will be tough explaining my absence, but of course I won't breathe a word."

The two released a relieved breath and thanked

her.

"Now," began Iviana, "I have some questions about this city—"

"Of course you do," interrupted Aedis. "We've been leading you to the very place that will supply the answers to most of the questions I imagine you have."

Iviana followed her guides up to the oldest looking building she had seen in the city yet and into a dimly lit room with a single table in the center of it. Upon that table lay a book.

"That text contains our early history, written by a man who was there when we were placed at the bottom of the sea. Let me find you a chair so you may read comfortably."

"I'll go," Merrick volunteered brightly, eager to serve the Chosen One.

Iviana lay her hand upon the book. It was beautiful and, like everything else in Atlantyss, like no book she had ever seen. It suddenly dawned on her that the paper she sought could be tucked somewhere within its pages. She looked it over eagerly.

"Here you are," said Merrick, returning with the chair.

"There. Now, have a seat," Aedis told her. "And

take your time. We will be waiting just outside."

The footsteps of the two echoed as they left the dim room and Iviana looked about her. It was a strangely large room for just one book and its table. The book itself appeared as aged as the outside of the building and emitted a sort of sweet, musty fragrance.

Opening the book's thick cover, Iviana began to read...

This text I have written so for generations to come there may be no disputing our purpose beneath the ocean. It is my intention that this city shall never lose sight of its destiny. We were chosen by the Great One for a special purpose. Because our great Island Leader offered the Great One an obedient heart, we were chosen from every island in the whole of the Greater Archipelagos and we must always remember it was his humility and selflessness that has allowed this city to live in a way that most can only dream.

Our venture began with that great Island Leader, Milot, just before the death of our greatest Realm Leader, Latos. Milot was the Island Leader of Atlantyss before this city was moved into the ocean. He was a Seer and good friend of the Great One.

From the time Milot was a boy, he received insight from the Great One of what was to come. When he was finally appointed Island Leader, he was well prepared.

Milot had been informed that, after Latos death, the laws and restraints placed on the gifts given by the Great One would be far heavier than they had previously been. He was told they would be nearly suffocating and the Great One wanted Milot to prepare the people of our island for a season in which we would be hidden and set aside for a greater purpose. He said that when the day came when He would raise our island, we would be used greatly in the revolution that is, one day, to come.

Thankfully, the people of our island loved him greatly. When he warned the people what was to come and asked them to prepare, there was little argument. We promised we would surely do whatever the Great One asked—that we would go wherever He led us. In fact, we did not lose a single citizen over what was to occur, for Milot had been used to stir such passion that we truly were willing to do whatever the Great One wished.

So, the day came when the beginning of the Great One's plan was to take place. It is well remembered there was a flash of light before a giant, semi-transparent dome began to rise up from the borders of the island until it had covered us entirely. It was then the air quality changed and the light, as well, in a fashion. Then there was the rumbling. There was crashing and clanging of objects moving and falling and all were brought to their knees for we could not stand. It was certainly frightening, but altogether awe-inspiring. Suddenly, we saw the water rising over the protective dome and we knew we were being lowered. Before long, the entire dome was covered by the ocean of the Greater Archipelagos.

At last, our domed island settled on the ocean floor, though providentially not in the same area on the map in which it had been located before. Miraculously, everything that had crashed and broken was put right and it was as if nothing had happened at all, except we were no longer island dwellers, but sea dwellers. At first, it was quite frightening, for many wondered how we were to retrieve food, if we would run out of air or light, if we would ever see the sun or smell the breezes above, but we placed our faith in the Great One.

After some time, many began to lose heart, but then the dragons came and we learned it was possible to pass through the dome. From then on, the *dragons became our main transport, as few of our number at that time were Swimmers. Even so, we soon discovered no matter how much of our food supply was eaten, it never ran low, the oxygen remained plentiful and our new freedom began to accelerate and progress our community beneath the cover of water.*

So, we continue as we are, awaiting the day when the Great One will use us to move our land into its next age, when our gifts and ideals will be accepted by all. Until then, we place our trust and passion in the Great One, knowing that, one day, His promises to us will be fulfilled.

The text continued, but Iviana felt this was all she could take in for the time being. It was fantastic, to say the least. She had always thought the gifts and ways of the Greater Archipelagos were interesting, but to know what the realm *could* be was almost frustrating. She, too, anticipated the day when these people would be free to share their culture with the rest of the realm. They certainly seemed an ardent group, unlike the dead council lording over those above. How amazing were the Great One's ways that He would choose to hide a people within the water that they could be free until a day when they would lead the rest of the realm in all the Great One had taught them.

Standing, she sighed, somehow knowing the parchment she sought would not be found here. She thought perhaps her finding this place might have something to do with what the Great One wanted her to know, but what she sought was deeper even than this secret place.

Regretfully, she left the book where it was—wishing she had time to finish it—and met Aedis and Merrick where they waited for her.

"I feel very fortunate to have found this place," she told them quietly. "You are a truly impressive community. I can't wait until you are unleashed on the whole world."

Merrick blushed and Iviana realized how young he was despite his gawky height. He truly must be a genius of a boy if he was working as a Junior Kais. She wondered how many geniuses above were not being appreciated and used as they should be. In truth, it was hardening her heart further against the council's ways. This was something she would have to face at some point.

"Thank you, Iviana," said Aedis. "We, as I am certain you have observed, are truly honored to have been able to meet you at this time. We will share your words with the others for it will lift their spirits. Truly, it will."

Merrick looked at Iviana and opened and closed his mouth a few times before finally saying, "Don't be afraid of the gifts the Great One has given you. I know it can feel like a great responsibility for people so young as us three, but someday, I'm sure, we'll all meet again...and we will finally see everything come together."

Iviana was a little dumbfounded by the boy. "Thank you, Merrick. If ever I feel alone, I will remember you two. Oh, how I look forward to seeing all you achieve one day."

Aedis' eyes filled with unshed tears as she embraced Iviana. "I know you must leave soon and I am sorry for it. I feel that we have become fast friends."

Iviana shared her feelings. She felt she had so much in common with these people—that they were kindred spirits. "Well, there's no reason why I should leave just yet. I know I have friends waiting for me, but I cannot leave without seeing a little more. What else can you show me?"

"Oh, there is a lot more to be seen!" said Merrick excitedly.

Aedis pulled a foreign contraption from her

pocket and appeared to be checking for something. "Classes don't dismiss for another hour. What do you say we let her sit in on one?"

"I would love that!" Iviana exclaimed.

The three rushed through the city—the two young people pulling Iviana past sights she would have liked to look on longer—until they scurried a long building filled with all sorts of rooms. As Aedis led Iviana, she whispered they were taking her to one of the smaller classes so she would not be mobbed with attention.

"We should be just in time for a lecture on dreams," Aedis told her as they approached the door. "It doesn't aid in preparing one for most occupations, so it isn't one of the more popular classes, but there are always just enough students interested to keep it going. They say the great Island Leader, Milot, received most of his prophecies through dreams. That's why the class is offered at all."

Aedis finished her explanation when they entered the room where an entire class turned at the sound of her voice and stared, not at the one from whom it had been spoken, but at Iviana. Iviana only smiled. It was lucky she had met the Kais previously and been exposed to their awe of her and whatever it was she was expected to do, else she might have opted to leave.

"Caidence," Aedis said to the older woman in the middle of the room. "This is Iviana. You may have heard something of her appearance in our city?"

Caidence smiled broadly. "Of course."

"Would you mind if we sat in on your lecture?"

"Not in the least. Iviana, we are honored to have you. Please be seated anywhere you like and if you wish to add anything to what I am saying during the class, please feel free to do so." Iviana knew nothing about dream interpretation and couldn't imagine why this woman felt she would have anything to share on the matter, but she smiled humbly and nodded her understanding before sitting in the large, comfortable chair Aedis led her into.

Aedis couldn't have chosen a better lecture for her to attend had she known her for years, for it was one of the few classes she would not only have been able to understand, but would also be genuinely interested in. She had had numerous dreams that affected her more than she thought they should, but it had never occurred to her they could truly mean something. Growing up, she had dreamed of a large cedar with a dove perched on it and it had certainly surprised her when the vision had appeared in her waking life. But that was nothing to the dream she'd had some time ago of the sorceress, Aradia, rising up from the sea and setting a demonic fire after her. So much truth had been revealed through that dream that was relevant to her at the time and still she had never thought to pay more heed to her other dreams—to watch for messages from the Great One within them.

By the time the lecture ended, she had so many questions for Caidence, but any opportunity she may have had to ask them was stolen. For, just as the lecture ended, Aedis and Merrick took her by the hands and hustled out of the room just as a number of students made ready to rush her.

As they escaped through the door, around the corner and into a little room that contained cleaning supplies, Aedis explained, "I'm sorry. It's just that Chamaeleo wanted us to keep you from those that would overwhelm you and let me tell you, a bunch of excited eight to sixteen-year-olds would certainly do it."

"Oh, that's alright. I understand. Is there another lecture we can visit now? I want to hear more."

"That was the last hour of lectures, I'm afraid," Aedis replied regretfully. She peered out of the doorway before adding, "Alright. I think the coast is clear."

But just as they exited the room, a trio of older people approached them. The first of these, a middle-aged man with a glimmer of humor in his eyes, asked, "Aedis, Merrick, for what purpose did you have our visitor in a cleaning closet?"

Recognition registered on the faces of Iviana's guides as they saw who stood before them, followed closely by the deepest blushes she had ever seen.

"Er...um..." Aedis began, but seemingly unable to form an excuse she turned to Iviana, informing, "These are our Island Leaders, Ferrol"—she gestured to the man who had just spoken—"Jephran and Mae." The last of these was a duo of women. The first might have been in her early thirties and emanated strength and courage. The other was a gentle, much older woman with flowing white hair and kindly expression.

Iviana felt she ought to bow to the three, but before she could do so, *they* bowed before *her.*

"We offer you the highest honor we can afford," said Jephran as they knelt.

"If only to make you as uncomfortable as possible," added Ferrol with a wink as they straightened.

Iviana relaxed immediately. She would rather no

one felt the need to bow to a simple Seeker who lived in a cottage in another world and spent her days healing village folk and tending her garden and cow, but if they must do it, at least this man had the tact to do it with humor.

As Jephran sent a scowl at Ferrol for his comment, Mae stepped forward and surrounded Iviana in a tender embrace that Iviana wished she could experience every day.

When Mae pulled back—though only at arm's length so she could look into Iviana's face—she said, "You are a precious girl, Iviana...with a precious heart. Never mind our talk of what is to come and our show of honor; you are much more than your future. You are a beloved daughter of the Great One and so you are a beloved daughter of mine."

Tears pricked Iviana's eyes and one rogue tear ran down her cheek, but this was all the emotion she allowed herself to show in front of the group of strangers. A simple, "Thank you," squeaked from her mouth as the woman smoothed the stray hairs from Iviana's face before moving away. But still Mae's smile remained on her and Iviana thought the feeling of love washing through her might never fade.

Iviana hardly heard anything that was said during

the last of their meeting and muttered her goodbyes as Aedis and Merrick led her out of the building. All she could think about was that sweet woman and the warm feeling of belonging she had imparted into her spirit. She thought that was what Paradise with the Great One might feel like, only she had been blessed with a taste of it before death.

"Are you alright, Iviana?" Aedis asked with concern.

"Yes, of course."

"I'm sorry for having the Island Leaders sprung on you like that. Obviously, I had no idea they would be in the school. I suppose they were looking for you."

"And we wouldn't have taken you into the cleaning closet had we known," added Merrick with a grin of both embarrassment and mischief. It seemed he didn't altogether mind the mirth of the situation.

"Tell me, why do you have three Island Leaders?" asked Iviana. "All the other islands I know of only have one."

"Ah, well, our community does not lead the simple lives that those above do," Aedis explained. "There is so much done in a day that we find it helpful to have multiple leaders to oversee various aspects of the community's lives. There used to be a fourth leader, actually, but she left because she was called by the Great One to a mission in another realm. Most of us don't know much about it as the other realms are quite beyond us, but she is considered a hero around here."

Iviana had more questions she wished to ask, but was distracted by a man who was coming from around the corner of a nearby building.

"What is it?" Aedis asked, turning to where Iviana looked.

"*Marquen?*" Iviana called.

Marquen looked to where she stood, his expression changing from one of perplexity to pleasure. He raced across the road to join her.

"Marquen, what in the world are you doing here?" Iviana asked.

"Well, I could ask you the same thing, couldn't I?" he replied.

"I suppose, but..."

Marquen smirked and relented. "I'm pleased to find you well and with kind-looking people such as these. We were all quite worried about you, but Tragor came around noon—after we had frantically searched the shoreline—and gave us the impression you were alright. Though, how he can convey a message without words is rather uncanny. At any rate, the lot of us settled down after that, but, well, I was just too curious when Tragor wouldn't show us where you were. So...here I am...wherever this is..." He looked around, obviously delighted by what he saw.

"Yes, but Marquen, how did you get here? How did you *find* here?"

He looked into her eyes as if uncertain he would relay a secret. "I won't lie to you, of course. It's one of my gifts. I can 'teleport' from one place to another. I do this rarely, however, and I've never told anyone. I'm afraid the council would have some things to say about it as it is a gift that has never been seen before—as far as I know. It would certainly make them nervous. Anyway, I simply asked the Great One's gift to take me to you and I ended up on the other side of that building over there. I will say, this place is stunning...and entirely curious."

Iviana noticed Aedis and Merrick appeared concerned by his presence in their city when Aedis commented, "I think I need to go speak with someone."

"Of course," Iviana replied, then added, "Don't worry, Aedis. He is a good friend. He is *trustworthy*."

Aedis nodded and went on her way.

"Trustworthy?" asked Marquen? "Have I stumbled on something I shouldn't have?"

"Indeed," Iviana affirmed. She was attempting to decipher how the people would react to his appearance. She knew *she* was alright because she was part of some prophecy, but was Marquen a part of it? Would it matter if he wasn't? "Teleport, you say? It sounds about as fantastic as everything I've seen here. Hard to imagine keeping it to yourself."

"Mmm...yes, but, you see, the council did not altogether like it when they found out I possessed more than one gift. I was the first ever to have admitted I had more than one. That was why I entered into the solitude of the hills at the tender age of twelve, to be away from those who would call gifts given by the Great One a blasphemous thing. Unfortunately, many feel the same about your gifts. At any rate, as I said, they would not have been happy to learn of this one."

"Yes, I see you're right." She turned to Merrick as if to ask if it was alright she explain their current setting.

He seemed to know what she was going to ask and supplied, "I support whatever you believe is wise." He didn't look at all worried. Perhaps he liked Marquen or perhaps her words to Aedis had assured him.

Marquen raised an eyebrow.

"This is Atlantyss," she told him.

"Yes...I see. I recall the island having existed, oh, a hundred years ago, I suppose. But it disappeared at the time of Latos' death. It's become quite a mystery since then." He looked around him, taking it all in. "Are we under water?" he asked.

Iviana nodded.

"Interesting." He continued looking about. "Intriguing. I can see the Great One has been at work here all this time. I've never seen anything like it. It's astonishing."

Iviana nodded with a pleased grin. "You have no idea."

Aedis returned and informed, "They say you may handle the situation however you see fit, Iviana."

Iviana blushed and glanced at Marquen who raised smiling brows at her. She didn't know what he was thinking, but she could guess. "There is a prophecy," she informed him.

"I do not doubt it. I expect there have been many."

"I suppose it is late," said Iviana, giving her surroundings a final glance. "We should be getting back."

Having said her good-byes, Iviana turned to Marquen and realized they needed a way back, as she did not know where Tragor was to be found, but before she could say so, Marquen took hold of her arm and, in a flash of light, they appeared just outside the cave where her friends awaited her return.

"Iviana, where have you been?!" Nimua shouted when she spotted them a few moments after they appeared.

"Good gracious, dragon lady, we've been worried sick over you," Flynn added a little annoyed, but obviously relieved.

"I'm so sorry. I—" Suddenly she remembered she could not tell them where she had been. "I found a statue of my great-grandfather, Latos."

"Yes," Darist put in, his arms crossed. "I saw it too, but I didn't see you there."

"I found her doing a bit of exploring," Marquen said in such a way that closed the conversation.

"Well," Nimua said in a huff, "next time leave a note."

❧ 5 ❧

THE TRAVELERS CHOSE to remain on the island and continue on first thing in the morning. Iviana enjoyed a large dinner to make up for not having eaten during her eventful day and afterward decided to walk along the beach until the others had fallen asleep. She didn't want to risk their prying any information out of her about where she had been. Unable to keep from thinking about Atlantyss, she'd nearly slipped the secret during dinner.

The evening was brisk and pleasing as it always was in the Greater Archipelagos, the sky glistening with thousands of stars. She remembered her first night spent in this world and just how overcome she had been with its beauty. The only difference tonight was the moon glowed even brighter. Iviana felt she could race to the end of the beach, take a great leap and land on its silver surface.

Despite these pleasant thoughts, she worried over her lack of guidance from the Seeker's fire. Perhaps Rhimesh had been wrong. Maybe she wasn't supposed to be looking for a parchment.

Oh, I don't know.

Her feet led her to the water's edge. The slow, rolling waves were cool, but not cold, and it calmed her. "Great One, I know You're there and I know You care for me. Why won't You show me the way? Was I wrong to take this journey? Was I supposed to have gone alone, perhaps?"

A soft breeze tossed her hair and she was certain there was a presence within it, but she heard no answer. Pacing the beach, she waited, but for nearly an hour she heard no reply. Still, she waited until fatigue overwhelmed her and she stretched out on the sand.

It was the sun's first dawning rays that awoke Iviana on the seashore. As soon as she realized what she'd done, she leaped to her feet and raced toward the cave. She feared her late night stroll may have caused her friends to worry about her...again. A long lecture from Nimua was certainly in order and Flynn would give her one of his piercing expressions, but wouldn't say a word.

Making her way through the trees and into the

cave she shouted, "Nimua! Everyone, I'm sorry. I'm alright..."

Not a noise could be heard nor was there any movement.

"Are you seriously still sleeping?" she called out. Her voice wavered as she realized there was nothing in the cave but the belongings they had brought with them. Her mind racing, it dawned on her they must be out looking for her. Still, it was odd not one of them had stayed in the camp, if not to be there when she returned, then to begin packing.

That was when she noticed the plethora of footprints outside the cave. There was no way she and her companions had formed them all. Her heart began to race until her eyes found their way to a trail of footprints leading away from the cave.

Her stomach looped. It was then she remembered Chamaeleo's warning about the island, urging her to leave it as soon as possible. How foolish she had been to forget such a warning. What might now have happened to her friends? Chamaeleo had not been specific in her caution. What was she to do?

How she wished she might find Tragor, but he and the other dragons had not yet returned. The night before, she had assumed they meant to stay the night in Atlantyss and would return the following morning, but they were nowhere to be seen.

Desperately searching for what to do, she looked over the path of footprints as the fact there were others on this island sunk in. Somehow, it hadn't sound as if the Atlantians knew about them. If this was the case, what sort of people were they? Iviana followed the trail.

Here and there were feathers, beads and flowers she assumed had dropped from the bodies of the people who inhabited this island—the people who had taken her friends. It was altogether possible they had gone with this secret people willingly...but she couldn't believe they would go without her.

She hated thinking they had truly been abducted. Who knew what condition she would find them in if she could find them before *she* was found? The further she went, the more she regretted not waiting for Tragor. He could have flown her over the island much faster than she could find anything on foot.

Soon, the sandy ground grew rockier until it was apparent she was making her way into mountainous terrain. This was going to become a bigger problem than the time she was losing by walking. She wasn't a tracker...and the trail of footprints was fading fast as the sand faded.

Eventually, she was winding around the

mountain, a cliff's edge to her left, until all obvious signs of the trail ceased almost abruptly—so abruptly, she wondered if they had all stumbled over the cliff. Feeling sick, she peered over the edge and saw nothing but green and brown landscape below. She released a breath of relief.

"So, not that way..." she muttered looking down and then peering up the mountain. She couldn't imagine they had been able to climb that far with a group of kidnapped people.

At a loss for what to do, Iviana continued treading upward in hope of some enlightenment, but as she made her way around the bend, the strange cawing of an unfamiliar bird sounded overheard, catching her off guard and sending her off balance. Just as she had steadied herself, her foot caught on something that sent her stumbling backward down the path. Her body rolled uncontrollably until the incline was less severe and she was able to stop herself.

Slowly, she sat up and began checking for injuries when a pair of arms reached underneath hers and pulled her backward. Iviana screamed and fought against the arms that held her, but her captor was already releasing her. Leaping to her feet, she jumped about to discover a lone man standing in the space before her. Iviana looked him over, attempting to ascertain just what sort of man he was. He certainly had a rough appearance, unshaven with extremely tan skin; he didn't look to be much older than she was. His clothes were quite different from the garb normally worn in the Greater Archipelagos and he had a small silver earring dangling from one ear. Altogether, he looked a little like trouble.

"Good day to you," he said with a smirk. "I hope you realize I've just saved your life. A thank you is in order, I think, but of course if you don't care to give one..."

Iviana looked him over skeptically before following his gaze to the very edge of the cliff where a spot of her blood glistened on a rock.

The man nodded. "You had just about toppled over, sweetheart...so I don't suppose you'll mind my having grabbed you." When Iviana didn't respond, he continued, "Now, pardon my prying, but I am at an utter loss as to why you're standing on this particular island."

Iviana scowled at him. There was something flirtatious in his manner and everything in her disliked him. "I won't answer any questions until I know who you are."

The stranger raised his brow. "You're a spunky one, aren't you?"

Iviana wanted to roll her eyes, but had no idea what sort of danger she was in—whether or not this man had something to do with her friends' disappearance. She tried again, "I'm Ivi. You are...?"

The man chuckled. "Oh, alright. Necoli is my name." He stepped a little nearer. "Very pleased to make your acquaintance, Ivi...I suppose Ivi is short for something lovely, isn't it?"

Iviana blatantly backed away from him. "No, it's not. If you please, sir—"

"Necoli."

Iviana huffed inwardly. "Necoli. If *you* please—"

"I wish first for you to tell me what you are doing on this island."

The man stepped very close then, mere inches from her face. Iviana didn't like the intimacy of his action and thought she might run until she saw his hand rubbing the knife at his side. Oddly, she was relieved his only intention was pulling the blade on her. A weapon she could handle well enough.

The stranger noted where her eyes fell and stepped away again. "To tell you the truth," he said, "if it weren't for the fact your clothes are not of this world, I would have had the dagger on you before a word was spoken between us. Now, if you please—"

"I know, I know," Iviana interrupted, irritation

dripping from her words. "You want to know what I'm doing here. Truth is, I don't even know where 'here' is." Iviana paused a moment. Without knowing who this man was, she was uncertain how much she should reveal. Absently, she gripped the hilt of her sword. "I am traveling and stopped here to rest for the night." She watched his face, searching for any clues as to whether or not he knew anything about her friends.

Necoli gave her a doubtful glance. "You *are* a beauty. I would really hate to cause you any discomfort."

He had been slouching previously, but stood to his full height now. Iviana thought she would like to back further away from this large, muscular man as she gulped and sought a way to proceed.

Having read the consternation on her face, he reverted to the playful tone used previously. "I simply need the truth, Ivi girl."

But that was not the tone to take with her just then. Iviana glared up at him and allowed the fullness of her sudden vexation to light upon him. "I don't know who you are and, to be perfectly honest, I don't care. All I need to know is what you've done with my friends and I might just let you go unscathed. I demand you take me to them so we may be on our way."

Necoli searched her face for a long time, his expression unreadable. Iviana replied with an icy glare. She did not like being accused of lying. Moreover, she wanted to get her companions safely away from this place.

He released a sigh, rubbing the back of his neck. "Sheesh, beautiful, I do believe you mean it. Listen, I think we ought to come to an understanding. I'm not from this island...you're evidently not from this island. That, I believe, is the most important issue here."

"How so?"

"Because this island is...well, it's probably the closest thing we've got to hell in this world." His previously confident demeanor faltered as though he were frightened.

"Why do you say that?"

"You don't know, then? I see. Well, if you want to find your friends, you'd better get going and you'll need to watch your back." He thought for a moment before adding with a grin, "Better yet, I'll watch your back. I'm coming with you."

"You didn't have anything to do with their disappearance?" she asked, feeling a little thwarted. At least if he'd been one of the kidnappers, he would know where to find them.

"Don't look so disappointed, love. Shouldn't you be glad I haven't taken your friends?"

Iviana shook her head. "No, I just—" she touched her hand to her head, suddenly feeling a little lightheaded—probably from the fall she had taken some moments ago. "I just want to know where they are. I want to know if they're alright."

"Ah, well, I can assure you of one thing: they aren't. How do you know they were taken anyway? Why aren't you with them?"

Iviana, feeling faint, tried to listen for any nearby streams as she replied, "I fell asleep on the beach. My friends were camped elsewhere. When I returned this morning, they were gone. I was following a trail, but it vanished a while back."

"I see. Well, that isn't good."

Iviana felt overheated and ill. "What's the danger then?" she muttered.

"The inhabitants of this island are cannibals."

"Cannibals...?" She'd never heard the word before.

"They, uh...well, they consume human flesh."

Iviana gasped in disgust and disbelief as her vision grew dark. Slowly, she lowered herself to the ground, holding her head in her hands.

"Uh, are you alright?"

Iviana could barely hear his muted question. She shook her head and blinked, trying to clear her vision. "Water..." she whispered.

"Oh, sure. Just—just wait right here."

Iviana knew she was very near fainting and tried desperately to fight it. Not that she had never done so before. In fact, she knew she was quite prone to it and this was an intense irritation of hers; it had just never come on so slowly and now was not the time to be vulnerable. How was she to help her friends if she went around fainting? She fell back upon the ground, still grasping at consciousness. Just as a dark form approached her, she passed out.

Necoli looked down on her, uncertain of what to do. Her face was pale and blotchy and he thought perhaps the heat of the day with the added stress of her situation had been too much for her. His bluntness couldn't have helped either.

He looked at the cask of water in his hand and then dumped it over her face. When she didn't stir, he went back for more. Kneeling beside her, he held her head up and poured the water over the top of her face.

Iviana was awoken by the refreshingly cold water running down her neck. "That's it, girly. You're alright; just a little overheated," she heard someone say. Opening her eyes in search of the speaker, she quickly sat up. She regretted this action, however, when her head began throbbing.

Necoli realized she needed some space and left for more water.

"Here," he said, handing her the cask upon his return.

Iviana eyed it, then remembered he had gone to get her water before she'd fainted. "Thank you," she said between gulps.

Having finished the water, she soon felt better—well enough to stand, anyway, even if her head wasn't completely clear.

She reached down for the pack that had fallen from her back and started down the mountain, intent on finding her comrades. There had been something that made the situation direly urgent, but she couldn't recall what it was.

"Hey, wait a minute there, lady love," Necoli called. "Where are you off to so fast? You just fainted, you know. Besides, you're going to need my help with the cannibals."

Ah...that had been the issue. Iviana closed her eyes and then turned. "First of all, the nicknames end now. Secondly, I can handle this without any help from you. I've been in dangerous situations before."

Necoli burst into laughter. "I'm not saying you haven't, lass, but that doesn't mean you won't need help against a clan of cannibals. Trust me, you'll need me."

Iviana closed her weary eyes. She was irritated, but she was also very tired. "I suppose you know where they are?"

Necoli grinned. "There you go, love. That's better. Now, as a matter of fact, I believe I do."

Iviana stared up at him and shrugged. "After you, then."

Leading the way down the mountain, Necoli glanced over his shoulder from time to time, as if to be certain she was still there.

"Is it snack time or something?" she asked him flatly.

He tossed her another of his cocky grins. "How should I know? I'm just making certain you don't take off seeing as you dislike me and all."

"I'm too tired to dislike you right now," Iviana answered, though she knew this was untrue. She was just too tired to care that she disliked him. "I just want you to take me where I need to go."

He looked her over, then turned away, a little disappointed he hadn't gotten a rise out of her. He liked the gleam in her eyes when she was angry. It was then they arrived where the trail she had been following earlier ended.

"You want to see something grand?" he asked.

"Not really."

"*Oh*...then avert your eyes, snooty."

Iviana watched as he moved a large boulder away from the side of the mountain where the trail had ended. Sweat seethed from his forehead. Iviana knew if Darist had been there, it would have been nothing for him to move it. Still, the man must be awfully strong to have done it without Darist's gift. Seeing this display of strength made her second guess how safe she was with him. She felt she could defend herself against a weapon, but against such strength, she was in trouble.

"There you go," he said.

"What is this?" Iviana asked, looking into the large, black hole where the boulder had been.

"That's the entrance to their village—the swiftest way I know to get there anyway."

"How do you know where it is?"

"I was captured by them a few days ago. I'd only just escaped when I saw you tumbling down the mountain."

"Oh."

"Mhm. Lets get going, then."

Iviana stepped into the entrance of the dark cavity and thought she would really rather not try and make her way through it alone. Still, she didn't want to proceed any further with a stranger whose moral compass she couldn't be certain of. "Thank you. I should be fine on my own now."

"That's tough, sister. You go on in. I'll have to try and shimmy this rock back into place from the inside.

Silently, she stepped inside and ran her hand along the wall of the tunnel. She was certain it had been hand-carved and wondered how long it had taken. Next thing she knew, Necoli was holding a torch out to her, lighting it with flint and sword.

"Should we have a light? Won't we be spotted more easily?"

"You're certainly welcome to lead us through the dark, if you like. We may never get there, but it's up to you."

Iviana rolled her eyes. "Fine. Light it."

They moved through the dark, empty tunnels slowly, noiselessly, scarcely breathing for fear they'd be heard. Necoli led Iviana along with gestures and shrugs when he was uncertain of the way, for the eerily echoing tunnels offered numerous choices of direction and wound about within the mountain like a labyrinth. Often, Necoli simply offered another shrug and guessed on a direction. Iviana prayed he wouldn't get them completely lost. Secretly, she feared they would end up starving to death in the tunnels or, worse, eventually found and eaten by the island's inhabitants.

It was still difficult to believe that such people existed in the Greater Archipelagos. With all the rules and precautions, judgment and criticisms, how could the cannibalistic people live as they did? She dearly hoped the council was not at all aware of the island—especially not Flynn—for if it was known, they had ignored the sickly state of it. Still, she could not imagine that was the case and supposed it was something Flynn would handle with the council *when* she got her dear friends off this forsaken island and *when* they had found what they sought.

All the same, she was uncertain they would continue their mission after this. Her current trepidation made her consider taking them directly home. She could seek on her own then, if she felt it necessary. After all, the Great One was sending no signs. Perhaps it had not been His desire she seek the paper with shining inscription after all. Look at the mess it had gotten them into.

Necoli shot her another of his "lets try this way" shrugs as they came to another set of tunnels. But as they turned into the passage to the left, Iviana felt a fervent tug in her spirit to the right and turned to peer down that way. All she could see was darkness, but something about it was catching her.

Stepping toward it, she thought perhaps she had heard a call or moan, but couldn't be certain. As the feeling subsided, however, she assumed if she had heard anything it was probably something that would prepare her for dinner.

She flew after Necoli's fading light.

Still, she questioned what had happened as she followed him. It had lasted only moments, but had felt almost like her Seeker's fire. But if it had been her gift, why had it not continued to burn? She shook her head in an effort to shrug it off. She had not gotten the impression it would lead to her friends anyway and they were top priority.

Suddenly, Necoli took hold of her wrist and pulled her around the corner of another tunnel, stomping on the torch until it was out.

"What—" Iviana attempted to speak before Necoli slapped a hand over her mouth. For a moment, Iviana thought he was betraying her— possibly going to kill her—but then she heard an explanation in the form of approaching voices. Neither of them breathed as they waited for the islanders to pass. Iviana squeezed her eyes closed and prayed they wouldn't turn into their tunnel or shine a torch too closely. It would be a miracle if they didn't smell the smoke escaping from the dead torch, so she prayed for one.

It felt like an eternity before the group reached the passage where they were hidden. Iviana's heart beat wildly as the light illuminated the outline of Necoli's frame. *Please, no*, she prayed, for the group that was passing sounded quite large and, unless Necoli was better skilled in combat than she, she didn't think they would escape these strangers.

As the islanders passed, they were close enough Iviana could see they were of rough appearance and fairly mighty stature, but they continued forward without hesitation. Necoli uncovered her mouth, but still the two dared not move or breathe until they were certain the islanders were too far to hear any subtle movement.

"Well, that was a close one," Necoli commented easily.

Iviana glared at him. "Do you even know where we are?"

He shrugged and reached down to relight the

torch. "Fairly certain I do, but I'm not promising anything."

∞6∞

HIDING BEHIND A large boulder at the end of a tunnel, Iviana and Necoli peered over the village. With rays of sunlight shooting through holes in the thick blanket of vines and greenery that covered the entire village, it became clear why Iviana and her group had not seen it when they had flown over the island. From an aerial view, it would have looked like shrubbery, blending in with the landscape. Her eyes searched until she found the long, slim beams of wood around the border used as supports for the flourishing green tent. This place was obviously built to be concealed from the rest of the world.

It was certainly clever—too clever for the primitive tribe she had hoped would make up a cannibalistic society. But that hope had already been thwarted by the tunnel system in the mountain. Who knew how many of the mountains surrounding this valley were used as hidden entrances into the village?

Necoli, too, had given her the impression they were a primitive people. Whether or not he had done so by desire, she could not be sure. It would certainly make him dangerous if he had, but that could wait. She needed to come up with a plan to move through the village without being seen...before Necoli came up with his own foolish plan.

Presently, Necoli whispered, "Follow me."

Before Iviana could stop him, he sauntered out of the tunnel and into the village. Iviana sat down behind her rock, huffing angrily at the gall of this stranger. Of course, she was not going to follow him. He was leading her into certain death. She looked up. Was he truly leading her to her death? Perhaps the whole thing had been a ruse. If that were so, why would he have taken so much trouble to fool her into this place? Surely it would not have been difficult to carry her into the village when she was passed out.

Iviana peeked over the rock again. She saw him looking over a couple of large casks before glancing up at her with wide eyes, urging her to join him. He seemed innocent enough. Was he mad, then?

She heard noises coming from one of the tunnels

leading to the one she was in. Uncertain from which passage it came, she could not know how to hide herself. With another huff, she rolled her eyes, stood as though it was her perfect right to be there and walked out to meet Necoli.

He was pleased. "My lady, I thought you'd never come," he said, "and, see, I cannot decide which of these earthen vessels is best."

"What are we doing out here?" she asked with some irritation. "We won't go unnoticed for long."

"I'm not so sure." He proceeded to tussle Iviana's head of dark wavy hair. "With your dark hair, you really look just like one of them, if you'll look around you, and your clothes might have been stolen from one of your victims. As for me, well, if they happen to recognize me, don't stand too close. Better yet…" He snapped his fingers. "Take hold of my wrist as if you're escorting me somewhere after you've hunted me up. Yes, that should do it. In any case, shouldn't we find your beloved companions before they're roasted into some confection?"

A little disgusted, Iviana replied, "Ah, but as you've taken the initiative thus far, why not let me know what you think wisest so I may be aware of what action *not* to take and think up a plan that won't result in our joining them for a hardy meal."

"Oh, no, dearie, I'd definitely be dessert."

Iviana rolled her eyes.

"Now, you...you would be the spices." He laughed aloud. "That's good, isn't it? But don't get miffed with me just yet, sweetheart." He held up a warning finger before her face. "I've just been thinking up an idea. How would you like to turn me in?"

Iviana glared—not that she hated the idea entirely. "I'm sure this is going somewhere intelligent..."

"I knew you would. Like I said, you really look like one of them with your hair like that. I say you tie my wrists together, inform them you've 'found' me and say you'd like to put me with the others. It should lead us right to them."

"Don't you already know where they are? You said you were held captive here."

"Well...to be honest, they could be anywhere. It's not as if they have a kitchen and, to tell you the truth, I wasn't for eating. I was for marrying. Apparently one of the tribeswomen took a liking to me. Can't say I blame her, but I wasn't relishing sharing her diet for the rest of our days together; it just wouldn't have lasted."

While he talked, Iviana searched for a bit of rope.

When at last she found some, she pulled him behind one of the tents and turned him around so she could apply it to his wrists.

"I'm not going to tie it too tight in case you end up needing your hands."

"How thoughtful of you. Now, lets get out of hiding before you're spotted stealing me from my ex-fiancé."

Iviana took her sword from its sheath and poked it against his back. "Move on then," she said.

Necoli hopped forward and led her to one of the tribe leaders. Iviana hoped he knew what he was doing.

When they reached a portly, bald man, Necoli urged Iviana to speak up. But before she could, the leader turned to Necoli, saying, "You've been found. Good. But you won't be marrying one of ours—not now. You've earned a place at meal tonight."

Iviana stepped forward and forced the lump in her throat down into her chest. "I thought I would put him in with the others."

The man looked her over a long while and suddenly Iviana realized he knew she was not part of his tribe. She pulled the tip of her sword from Necoli's back and made ready to defend them when he interrupted her. "You caught this one?" he asked, gesturing to Necoli.

She froze and nodded.

He looked her over again, pleased. "You have done well for one of your age. I do not believe I have taken notice of you before. Rest assured, I'll have my eye on you from now on."

Iviana wasn't certain how to respond, so gave the bald man another nod.

"You're Nod's daughter?"

Iviana blinked, attempting to decide if it was wise to be Nod's daughter. She nodded again.

"Well, good girl. You may take this rat to the far tent."

Iviana responded by poking Necoli in the shoulder with her sword and moving wherever he moved since she had no idea where this "far tent" was.

"You've hit it off with the leader, Ivi girl," Necoli commented. "Who would have seen that coming? I'm guessing he's got you in mind for his next wife."

Iviana shuddered at the thought. "You know where we're going?"

He shrugged. "I think so."

Iviana really hoped so, but something else was

bothering her. "Necoli, that man seemed fairly intelligent."

"Did he? You telling me he's your type?"

"I just thought he'd be more...savage, you know?"

"Yes," Necoli replied with a sigh. "You would think so. I wish I could say I had an explanation, but I really only just discovered them. Whatever is going on, it is a sickeningly disgusting, treacherous business."

There was real emotion in his statement and Iviana wondered if he wasn't so bad after all—if he was perhaps more human than he wanted to appear. She was about to ask something of the sort when Necoli gave her a glance before entering one of the tents. Iviana looked about her and rushed in after him.

The moment the flap closed behind her, Necoli whispered, "Now!" and proceeded to knock out one of the two guards within the tent. Iviana's eyes widened as the other guard raised a weapon toward her. She quickly swiped up a nearby cask and smashed it over his head.

"Well done, love," Necoli commented.

Iviana rolled her eyes before she realized who was in the tent with them. Tied to posts were Flynn,

Darist, Marquen and Brenna.

"We've done it! We've found you!" Iviana whispered in delight.

"Thank the Great One, you're alright," Flynn whispered back. He looked up at the tall stranger. "Who's we?"

Iviana began untying the four from the wooden polls. "This is Necoli," she explained.

"And Necoli is a friend, I take it?" Darist queried.

Iviana shrugged. "For now. He's helping."

As Necoli stood freeing Brenna's arms from her ropes, he said, "I would gladly befriend you, you blonde beauty."

Flynn took careful notice of him then and turned an angry shade of red, but Iviana had just finished untying his arms, so he politely insisted Necoli handle Marquen's ropes while he finished with Brenna's.

"Where's Nimua?" Iviana gasped when she realized who was missing.

"It seems she's been chosen as a bride to one of the men," Marquen replied.

"Do you know where she is now?"

"I'm afraid not."

"I might be able to help with that," Necoli offered.

"Then spit it out," urged Iviana.

"When I was chosen as groom to one of the ladies here, it was to be a double wedding with a skinny little gray-haired man who, at the time, had not found a bride that suited him. Could it be the same man?"

"That's about what he looked like," Darist replied as Iviana broke the tight chains that held him. It seemed they'd discovered his gift. Iviana thought he probably could have freed himself of them anyway if it wouldn't have pulled the whole tent over them in the process, subsequently alerting the cannibals to their escape. "You know where they'd have her?" he asked Necoli hopefully.

"That I do."

As mad as this stranger drove her, Iviana was beginning to see his value. "What do you propose we do?"

∞

They escaped in a cloud of smoke. Though their flight was chaotic, Iviana was relieved they had escaped at all. Somewhere deep inside, in a place she hadn't acknowledged, she'd thought they were going to die on the island. Nevertheless, she now ran alongside Darist, Necoli and Nimua, who was still bound at the wrists and feet and was being carried like a precious babe in Necoli's arms. Iviana knew they would be moving faster if they had had time to untie her or if Darist had been able to get hold of her with his gift of strength as an aid, but Necoli had been swiftest when they'd been caught. And, though he was not so anointed with it, he had a good deal of natural strength that would have to do.

Flynn and Marquen had sneaked out earlier to search for the dragons and were supposed to meet them at the cave. They would hopefully be able to gather their supplies and track down the dragons in time to meet them on the beach. Iviana fervently prayed their far-fetched plan would come together.

"What do we do if Flynn and Marquen haven't found the dragons?" she asked through desperate breaths.

Necoli glanced at her as if she was crazy. "I wasn't aware there was a chance they wouldn't," he called back to her.

Iviana pressed her lips together. She was tired, but stopping wasn't an option. Even slowing meant immediate death. These people couldn't afford to have their island discovered by the realm. Iviana could only imagine what was to happen when Flynn returned to the council with this tale.

They had been spotted the moment they found Nimua and, in their escape, had mazed through tent after tent, but the thick vine-covered casing about the perimeters of the village offered no exit. With no alternative, Iviana had stolen a burning log from a passing fire-pit and headed toward one of the green walls. Tents and clotheslines were lit as she ran, for she went clumsily, uncertain what direction to take. She had only hoped the three behind her were able to keep ahead of the flames. She had heard them call often, at first wondering what she was planning and then cheering as they understood her intention.

Finally, she had caught sight of what she was after: the thick array of vines that made up the wall. The villagers were converging on either side of them and Iviana knocked a few aside with the fiery log in her hands. The fire had begun to burn her, but she continued forward until she reached her destination and lit it. The wall burst into flame, but soon burned enough space for the four to escape. They had run then, as swiftly as their legs would carry them.

Darist reached back and took Iviana's hand, practically pulling her arm from its socket in an effort to speed her up. Iviana wanted to cry out in pain, but was grateful; she didn't know if she could be counted on to push herself much longer. The men she ran with were much stronger than the average person and their speed was remarkable.

Finally, the cave was in sight, but upon entering, they found nothing had been packed and there was no sign of Flynn, Marquen or the dragons.

"Darist," Iviana breathed out, looking toward the empty shoreline.

"I know," he answered. "They'll get here. We just have to keep from getting captured before then."

This lifted Iviana's spirits a little. She prayed they had not been found, wherever they were. Each grabbed for a tent and pressed it flat, tossing their belongings onto the level surfaces. They then pulled the tents into large, lumpy sacks and threw them over their shoulders just as Necoli arrived with Nimua.

"Oh, happy day," said Necoli with a grin. "Now the cannibals won't have to collect it themselves."

Behind these two, Flynn and Marquen entered.

"Can't find the dragons," Flynn spat between breaths. "The islanders are close. We have to move."

Brilliant, thought Iviana.

They were trapped.

Nimua demanded she be untied, but they had no

time. The islanders' speedy approach was filled with boisterous shouts as the group raced from the cave. Iviana's heart sank at the sight of them not far behind when suddenly she felt something awaken inside her: the Seeker's fire. Though it was not as fervent as in the past, it was *present* and it would possibly save their tails.

Racing ahead of the others, Iviana urged them to follow as she flew with new vigor, fueled by the fire. Though the others were baffled, they followed without question in an effort to flee the cannibals.

A few more minutes of the exhausting race and a sharp left had them safely hidden in the cleft of a giant boulder. The group listened in silence as their pursuers continued past them, but Iviana turned away, searching for whatever the fire had led her to. There, within the cleft of the boulder, was a small door. The burning grew fierce as she gazed at the antiquated wood with artistic hinges and plain brass doorknob that was eerily familiar, though she could not say why.

Unable to control her curiosity, she tried the doorknob and, though it turned freely in her hand, the door did not swing open as it should. Sparks flew from the knob when she touched it and, knowing she should question this, she didn't. She simply pulled harder on the door, feeling it wanted her to open it, whether or not the rock it was built into was as happy at her tugging.

Finally, she drew her sword from its sheath and carved a little space between the ground and door, cutting at the solid clods of dirt and stubborn, dead roots until she was sure the door would open freely.

It did.

ༀ 7 ༃

TVIANA PEEKED INSIDE, but was startled by the presence of a dark shadow over her shoulder. When she turned, however, her friends were still peering out the crack in the rock as the cannibals passed. She questioned the darkness, but it had come and gone as quickly as she had noticed its existence and there was no time to contemplate it further.

She bent to crawl through the door and into a tunnel that sloped downward, seemingly leading to nowhere, but one more step to examine a piece of slate hanging at the very end and she was no longer in the tunnel.

"Oh, wonderful," she muttered grimly as she realized she had somehow transported to another place. With no clue as to where she was, it was disorienting, to say the least. She had wanted to escape the island, but ending up in the middle of nowhere wasn't an alternative she would have chosen.

As she turned to examine her surroundings, there was nothing but dry, rocky wasteland as far as the eye could see. Everything she viewed was a rusty brown hue and the ground felt like hardened clay beneath her feet. The sky retired overhead in sleepy violet hues, alerting her that dusk was descending.

Iviana grew distressed as she realized there was no way for her to return to the others. Sitting on the dry, dusty ground, she attempted to work out the occurrence and determined she must have traveled through a portal similar to the one in Jaela's Cavern. Upon that conclusion, a shiver crawled up her spine. She hoped she was not in some other unknown realm—especially one that looked like this deserted place. She bit her lip, praying the others would not follow her when they discovered her disappearance.

Flynn was the first to take notice of her absence, however, evident by his appearance at her side.

"What are you doing here?" Iviana shouted at him with a good punch to the arm.

"*Ouch!* Where are we?" He looked about curiously, but she did not answer his question, watching the wheels in his head turn as hers had. He looked at Iviana. "We're not in the Greater Archipelagos anymore, are we?"

Iviana smirked. "You think?"

"Well, how was I supposed to know? You sure didn't leave any sign behind to keep us from following your mistake."

"*My mistake?* I'm sorry I didn't realize there was an invisible portal at the end of some underground tunnel. Had I, I assure you I'd have left a little note behind."

Flynn was quiet a while before, "I apologize. I shouldn't have said that."

Iviana was facing the landscape, her back to him. She had been ready not to forgive him, but sighed. "It's alright. I'm sorry I punched you..."

Flynn smiled. "So...you think the others will join us?"

Iviana grimaced. "I hope not."

A moment later, she added, "I followed my Seeker's fire." Though she left out the fact it had fled her.

Flynn perked up. "Then we're supposed to be here...wherever here is. I don't suppose you have any idea—"

"Your guess is as good as mine."

Flynn shrugged. "The sky's kinda pretty, I guess."

"Where am I?" whispered an astonished voice.

Iviana and Flynn jumped and turned to see who had spoken.

"Brenna," said Iviana. "I was hoping no one else would come through."

"Uh...right. I'm fairly certain we'll all be together soon enough," she answered wryly.

"Maybe someone will get the hint when we don't return for them," Flynn said half hopefully, half ironically.

It didn't take long for Brenna's words to come to pass.

Next came Marquen. "A portal," he said when he realized he wasn't in the little tunnel anymore.

The three smiled.

Shortly after, Darist followed, informing that Nimua and Necoli weren't far behind him.

"Good!" Iviana said happily. "I suppose they'll have seen you disappear and know to turn back."

In the next moment, the two appeared beside them.

" *Why did you come?*" Iviana exclaimed, giving Nimua a little shake.

Nimua offered an ornery grin. "I wasn't going to be left out."

"And I certainly didn't come of my own accord," Necoli offered, "though I can't say being pulled along by a captivating woman is worth complaining about."

"I didn't want to go by myself," Nimua explained. She looked about her with interest. "This is exciting. I've never been outside the Greater Archipelagos." Her smile faded. "We can get back, right?"

Flynn and Iviana exchanged glances.

"We're not entirely certain," Flynn replied.

Nimua sat down and looked as if she was about to cry.

"Well, we aren't going to find a way just sitting around here," Marquen said matter-of-factly. "I propose we get moving."

"Right," Flynn agreed. "Anyway, we're not in any trouble. Ivi says she followed her gift here. I'm sure we'll find a way back when the time comes. Once we've found what we're looking for, she can use her gift to take us home."

Marquen looked into Iviana's face, but she avoided his gaze. She knew he guessed what was going on in her mind.

"Why don't we camp here for the night." Darist suggested.

Flynn disagreed. "I'd feel better if we covered a little ground—get a little more familiar with the territory. Ivi?"

Necoli burst into laughter.

Wearily, Iviana turned toward him, awaiting an explanation.

"Excuse me, friend," Flynn interrupted. "What is so funny?"

"You realize where we are, right?" Necoli asked.

Iviana looked around. It did look mildly familiar, but could their luck really be that good?

"We're on Kaern," Flynn muttered his realization. "And in Kierelia, if I'm not mistaken."

"Oh, thank the Great One," Iviana gasped.

"Kierelia?" Darist looked at her hopefully.

Iviana nodded.

Darist smiled and was about to say something when Nimua hugged Iviana with glee. "I've so wished I could see your world!" she exclaimed. "Now, here we are!" As she turned to look about at the surrounding scenery, her excitement diminished. "But it's so...ugly."

Laughing, Iviana replied, "Not all of it looks like this. This is just a bit of wilderness. If we can find our way out of it, I think you'll see some very pretty landscape."

"Then lets not wait any longer," Darist said merrily. "Lead the way."

Iviana frowned. She was certain if Tragor were here he'd know which way to go, but he and the other dragons had been left in the Greater Archipelagos—probably with the Atlantians.

Necoli broke into her thoughts. "I think I've got this," he informed a little cockily and started forward.

The rest followed.

"Necoli?" said Iviana, running up to join him in the lead. "How are you so familiar with Kierelia?"

"I've traveled a lot."

"Oh. I hadn't realized you'd been outside the Greater Archipelagos."

He shrugged. Then a smirk spread across his face. "Why you so interested, Ivi girl?"

Iviana blushed. "My curiosity is perfectly natural. Not everyone crosses worlds. In fact, I understand very few do. I hadn't realized you were one of them—that's all."

"Well, I reckon there's a lot you don't know about me."

"Of course." In that moment, Iviana regretted not having lost him on the island, but supposed it was worth it if he could lead them out of the wilderness. She tried to remind herself how he had helped rescue her friends and even had to admit she couldn't have done it without him. "Necoli, I have to thank you," she said.

"I'm sorry you feel that way."

Iviana realized her face was contorted, revealing her difficulty in saying it.

"How long before we arrive in the pretty parts?" Nimua asked, having joined them in the lead.

Iviana smiled at her friend, suddenly eager to show off her home world.

"Not long now, lovely," replied Necoli.

Nimua and Iviana exchanged glances as Iviana rolled her eyes, but Nimua looked as if she was pondering something, then answered, "We're so grateful to you for helping us. I realize it was awful of me to pull you along with me. This isn't your mission after all."

Necoli looked up. "We're on a mission, eh? I confess I had been wondering what we were playing at."

"Well, it's Ivi's mission actually." Iviana tried to get her attention in order to stop her, but Nimua refused to notice. "We're looking for something, you see, and she's a Seeker."

Necoli was genuinely surprised at that. "*The* Seeker? Well, I have heard tales of you and I'm pleased to have been able to meet you."

Iviana listened for notes of sarcasm or flirtation, but could recognize none. She was a little speechless.

"We *are* proud of her," Nimua replied, as if Iviana was family.

"But I heard our Seeker disappeared some time ago."

Iviana opened her mouth to respond, but Nimua stopped her. "Iviana lives in this world—in this kingdom as a matter of fact. She had returned home is all."

"Oh, of course. I had heard she was from another world. Why, that was the issue entirely, wasn't it? That she had appeared from another world claiming gifts of the Great One. It's what makes her so interesting to gossiping tongues."

Iviana frowned. She really hated the gossip.

"Oh, the gossip's faded now," Nimua put in for Iviana's sake. "In fact, I think she's rather more old news, wouldn't you say?"

Necoli caught on to Nimua's hint and nodded. "I suppose so. I only returned to the Greater Archipelagos recently, so it was a fine, old tale to learn upon my arrival."

Iviana looked up. "Where were you before?"

"Here, of course."

"Don't you find it interesting we have three in our party familiar with our connected worlds?" asked Nimua. "I suppose I'm one of you, now. I think this could very well be life-changing."

Iviana watched as Necoli looked back at Nimua and smiled in a way that was actually quite sweet. That smile frightened her.

ॐ

It had grown terribly dark by the time they entered the outskirts of a forest and they had only to find a large, comfortable space to make camp. But Iviana felt certain she'd been hearing something following within the trees to their left. It appeared Darist had noticed as well as he shot a meaningful look her way. She was glad he did not say anything, not wishing to alert the others yet. She made her way nearer to try and catch a glimpse, but, though Marquen held a makeshift torch, it would be almost impossible to see what it was in the dark. Darist stepped up behind her, having read her thoughts.

"What are the two of you looking at?" Nimua asked, startling the two.

Darist silently put a finger to his lips.

Then, even more suddenly than Nimua's outburst, a large hairy creature leaped from the woods directly onto Necoli—who was in the rear by this time—knocking him to the ground.

Iviana and Flynn—the only two with weapons—pulled the swords from their sheaths and flew toward the beast. Flynn made ready to give the animal a good kick and make his cut when Necoli sat up with an astonished expression.

A large wolf sat licking his cheek.

"Just a moment, friends!" Necoli called.

"You...know this wolf?" Iviana asked, eying the beast.

Necoli turned and looked into the face of the animal and burst out in boisterous laughter. The animal stood aside and allowed Necoli to his feet.

"That I do," he said with a smirk. "Let me introduce you to my grandmother."

Brenna gasped as Flynn and Iviana turned to where the wolf was. However, it was not a wolf they saw standing there, but a tall, graceful woman—a woman Iviana knew.

"Chamaeleo..." she spoke in astonishment when Marquen held the torch nearer her face. She felt she was always to be surprised by the woman's appearances.

Chamaeleo threw her head back and released her beautifully congenial laugh. "Yes, it is I," said she. "I apologize profusely for having startled you. You see, I'd caught sight of you all a while back and I suppose it wasn't the wisest guise in which to have entered your armed party, but I couldn't help giving my grandson a bit of a fright. You understand, don't you?"

Iviana could not wrap her mind around the thought of this stunning woman, with long flowing brown hair and stunning brown eyes having been the hairy wolf.

"I don't understand at all," she gasped.

Necoli looked to his grandmother, pleased. Iviana had not yet seen him look so pleased or, if possible, so ornery. "She's a Shifter," he explained.

"Oh, I have heard of those from our history, but I've certainly never met one..." Nimua burst out. She looked upon the woman with great interest.

"What's a Shifter?" Iviana asked.

131

Necoli stepped in again. "She can take different forms, from various people to all types of animals and, every now and then, even plant life—really, just about whatever you can think of."

"H—how?" Iviana stammered.

Chamaeleo shrugged. "It isn't complicated. I think of what I want to be or how I want to look and I take the shape. It's one of the Great Gifts. As you know, they don't always make sense in the natural mind, but they don't have to."

Iviana wasn't convinced she understood the situation and was glad when Darist said for her, "Good woman, I don't mean to sound impertinent, but you look awfully...vivacious...How in the world are you Necoli's *grandmother*?"

Chamaeleo, who appeared to be only in her thirties or forties, replied with a sparkling grin, "As I said, I am a Shifter."

"So, this isn't your natural form?" Nimua asked. Iviana thought Nimua was the only person who could ask such a question without sounding rude.

Chamaeleo shook her head.

"But why take this form?" Nimua inquired again.

Chamaeleo thought a moment. "When people see an old woman, they expect her to be, well, old and they treat her thus. I do not feel my age and I would like to be treated like a human. Besides that, I may be a little vain, I suppose. At any rate, this isn't the only form I take, though it is the most common of late."

"Wait a moment, Granny," Necoli broke in. "How does *Ivi* know you?"

Iviana met Chamaeleo's eyes and waited for the woman to respond, hoping she would not reveal the complete truth. She didn't want everyone to know there was some prophesy about her. Being the only Seeker was enough pressure.

"Oh, we've run into one another a time or two," she answered. It was obvious to everyone there was more than the woman let on, but Iviana didn't care. She was grateful her secret had been kept.

Suddenly, there could be heard a great band of horses galloping in the distance. Chamaeleo's attention was drawn by the sound of them and she squinted in the direction from which it was coming. Turning to the group, she said, "I really hate to chat and dash, but I've, uh…an appointment elsewhere. I will follow your trail and meet with you all again later, if I get the chance."

"Wait, Granny," Necoli uttered, but in moments Chamaeleo was a wolf again, leaping into the woods.

ೞ 8 ೞ

ONCE THEY HAD found a comfortable campsite, it wasn't long before the travelers were eating together around an open fire. Necoli had led them into a thicker wood than the one they had originally found and the group had been able to scavenge for edibles to add to the few supplies they had left.

Iviana finished her meal and read contentedly by firelight. Her choice of book was one she had forgotten until she'd discovered it in her pack—a token from her previous journey. She recalled the eccentric, kindly woman who kept a den of various birds behind her book shop. Iviana hadn't known many people before her, but she'd certainly never met anyone like her since. Handing Iviana the book, Bell had said by taking it, Iviana would be helping her free space for other books. As Iviana read, she doubted it had truly been the case, for the book she had been given was extremely diverting, despite its rugged appearance, and she was unable to put it down.

The man about whom she read was a little like herself in some ways and not at all in others. He seemed to be unwaveringly confident and self-assured—traits Iviana felt she lacked much of the time—but he appeared to be some sort of Healer. It seemed all one woman had to do was grasp the edge of his garment and she received her healing. Iviana could not heal so instantaneously and wondered if the book was only a made-up story. She wished she could go to the woman who'd given her the book and ask a little more about it. Perhaps another time she could make the trip.

Iviana was utterly absorbed by a tale of the miracle man multiplying a small meal into enough food for thousands when Darist and Marquen sat beside her.

"What is this book that has you so enthralled?" Darist asked her.

"Oh, I'm afraid it hasn't got a title," Iviana replied, "but it's full of countless stories. I think the tales might be a history of some sort...or perhaps only legend."

"Mm," Marquen murmured as he took hold of the book she held out to him. "My, it *is* old, isn't it?

And, you're right; it has no title. How peculiar. Do you mind if I read a little?"

Iviana gave her consent and turned to speak with Darist.

"So your Seeker's fire kicked in, eh?" Darist inquired.

"Yes," she replied happily. "I was beginning to get a little worried—wait! How did you know...?"

"I guessed. You just seemed so preoccupied. I knew it would spark up eventually, though."

"How could you be so sure?"

He shrugged.

Iviana looked her friend over. "You know, I've never known you to be so good at reading people."

"I wouldn't say I am. Maybe you just wear your thoughts on your sleeve?"

"Oh, dear, I hope not. That would be an uncomfortable existence. No use in keeping a diary if all my secret thoughts are known."

Darist smiled at her kindly. "Don't worry. To be perfectly honest, there are many times I can't read you at all."

They were interrupted by the sound of excited conversation. She and Darist looked to its source to find it had come from the mouths of Nimua and Necoli who sat together on the other side of the fire.

"Well, I would never have believed that roguish fellow could make good conversation," Iviana muttered in her surprise at seeing her good friend enjoying the company of such a man.

Darist did not immediately reply and Iviana looked into his face to see if she could read *his* thoughts. He did look meditative, but she wasn't certain she could guess what he was thinking. His face was a series of expressions.

He turned to her. "Well, I can't say I disagree with you, but perhaps there's more to him than meets the eye."

Iviana continued to watch the two together. "Perhaps."

ॐ

That evening, Iviana lay sleeping in her tent when she was awoken by the fluttering of wings outside. Curious, she sat up and pulled the tent flap aside and perched upon a piece of wood within the lightly burning campfire was the perfectly white dove she'd met several times previously.

He pointedly peered into her face, then flew off again only to land on the tent the men were using.

Groggily, she pulled herself out of bed and went after him. As she reached the bird, it proceeded to fly to a tree a short distance away. Iviana followed and continued this game of cat and mouse—uncertain as to who was the cat and who was the mouse—until she found herself before a lake thick with fog. She watched as the dove held itself in the space before the water to give her one last, daring glance, then flew into the mist.

Uncertainly, she watched its form disappear until her attention was pulled elsewhere. She sensed a malicious presence lurking behind her, but the feeling completely fled as she turned about to look for it. It was similar to the one she had sensed in the crevice of the rock on the cannibal island.

Iviana returned her attention to the lake and decided she was either sleep-walking or under a spell, for without another thought, she stepped into the mist and let her feet touch upon the surface of the water. Continuing to walk without sinking, she wondered how it was possible and hoped to catch another glimpse of the curious bird.

As the blanket of mist began to dissipate, Iviana found herself standing on a hill. The purple-gray sky above twisted and toiled and the air was thick with atmospheric conflict, as though some evil meant to claim it but was waylaid by the undercurrent of ageless glories. The ground vibrated lightly beneath her feet as goosebumps flooded her skin.

Iviana analyzed her surroundings, attempting to configure her location. Somehow, she knew she was no longer in Kierelia, but had no idea how she had entered this place. Even so, she was unafraid. The dove was with her, she knew, though he was not in sight. She felt him with her as an invisible confidant.

Gazing into the distance, she saw the only people within sight were gathered in one place, but she was too far away to make out their purpose. Immediately, her legs started in that direction as her Seeker's urgency burned within. She ran as swiftly as a deer, frolicking, almost floating, over empty space and landing effortlessly upon her feet.

Finally, she could just make out what the people were focused on. It was a man, though he barely resembled a man, he was so beaten and bloodied. He carried something over his back that looked to be extremely heavy for any man, let alone one so battered.

Iviana's heart stopped at the sight of him and then beat rapidly. Whatever was going on, it was wrong, she knew. What had this man done to deserve this? She squinted her eyes to better view what he dragged with him and discovered it was two beams of wood. Certainly, they were large and therefore heavy, but it made no sense to her.

She had paused her sprint to study the scene but now allowed her feet to carry her nearer the crowd until she was among them, though they did not take notice of her; she was like a phantom in their midst. Making her way to the forefront of the crowd, she beheld the beaten man. He was now laid over the planks of wood he had been carrying, his arms stretched out over a horizontal beam. She wondered what they could be playing at until she noticed a large metal spike glimmer in the hand of a man who held what looked like a hammer in the other.

She gasped, her hand clapping over her mouth in disbelief. Surely they were not going to...

"*This is the Anointed One, Iviana. He is the beloved of the Great One*," the spirit-dove whispered.

Somehow, Iviana knew this was the man she had been reading about in her book earlier that evening. He was the Healer, the one who lived with a love so revolutionary it moved her to her very core. This man, beloved of her Great Friend—here he was before her and...

No!!! her mind shouted. *No, no, no...it cannot*

be. They're not going to...

The man with the spike and hammer knelt beside the Anointed One, held the nail over his flesh and raised the hammer.

"*Nooo*!" Iviana screamed. She fell to her knees as the hammer came down and knocked the nail into the beloved of the Great One.

Something pulsed in the atmosphere, rocking Iviana as she attempted to scramble toward him to protect him and to stop these monsters. But she was held fast to the ground by some unseen force and could not get even an inch nearer him.

Iviana watched in horror as they continued nailing his body to the torturous configuration of wood while the crowd jeered. His face grimacing in wretched pain, she heard his miserable cries and felt his heart shattering.

Weeping from the depths of her heart, Iviana clutched her sick stomach and attempted to decipher what justice could possibly be involved in this. She screamed at the people with what was left of her voice, "How could you do this? This man is innocent! Please, *someone*, have mercy on him!" But no one heard her pleading.

Her attempts to stop the crowd futile, she returned her focus to the Anointed One. The beams were being maneuvered upright by a number of the people while the Anointed One screamed in agony, his pain ultimately ignored. When at last they had finished, his discomfort was only intensified as his body was forced to hang from the ropes and nails that held him. It was apparent breathing was not only difficult but harrowing and his face was contorted with indescribable suffering.

With sudden force, Iviana purged the contents of her stomach.

But this would not do. She forced herself to look up into his face and there he met her gaze, his eyes boring into hers until she felt the Seeker's fire blaze and crackle within her veins. She could see in her peripheral vision the green fire glowing through her skin, but nothing mattered except his eyes on hers, thanking her for being there with him, though she did nothing.

Iviana's eyes flooded again, but she blinked the tears away, refusing to let them blur her vision. She would not leave him alone...for that was what he was: alone, abandoned, hated and despised. Yet he did not return the people's hatred. He longed for them.

For whatever unimaginable reason, his face raw and bloodied, his body torn open in places, blood cloaking his body as a veil, earth clinging in every wound, he *wanted* them. Even as she could not help but admire him, it made her ill.

At last, he tore his gaze from hers and looked to the toiling sky above, the clouds having grown almost red as his blood, and cried to the Great One as a child might plead with his father, *"Why have you forsaken me?"*

As tears raced down her cheeks, Iviana waited, hoped and prayed.

But there was nothing.

Though the sounds of the crowd persisted, all was silent for Iviana and the Anointed One; that silence spoke volumes. He *was* abandoned to his fate and Iviana could take it no longer. Drawing to a stand, she attempted to rip herself from whatever held her that she might free him from his cruel torment. Though she knew it was too late to save him, she wished only that he might pass from this world in peace—that his death would not be a spectacle to be mocked. However, whatever grasped her was stronger than she—insistent—and she could move no more than before.

That was when she saw him—the one who was like a dark void as he moved amidst the crowd, invisible, as she was. The only difference was he did not see her as she saw him. But she could perceive from the expression on his face that it had been *his* plan to destroy this innocent man, that his dearest dream was coming to pass in these moments.

Then, as it became apparent the Anointed One was drawing his final breaths, the glorying joy on the face of the dark being hesitated, for as Iviana turned back to the Anointed One, his body began to crackle and light up, as if whatever power inside him was escaping. Though none but Iviana and the dark one saw this, it was evident the power fleeing from the dying body meant something to the dark creature and he was struck with sudden terror.

As if drawn down by the power in the body of the Anointed One, the clouds above released a startling bolt that struck the ground not far from the creature. With it, another pulse of atmospheric change coursed over the region, deepening the vibration underfoot. With that, the dark one fled as swiftly as if he had never been there.

As the clouds continued to curl and thrash overhead, the sparks of glory fleeing the Anointed One's body were nearly blinding and Iviana struggled to see if his lungs still moved. Even so, Iviana heard him utter his final words, "It is done."

As the ground began to tremble to the point that

others could feel it, the sky continued to strike the earth with its electric bolts and the crowd grew fearful, at last recognizing the closing of this life was unlike any other, and they fled.

Iviana had no interest in running. Though she had thought every tear within her shed, she sobbed harder than ever before. To the Great One she cried, " *Why?* Why have you let this happen? Why did you not let me help him?! For what purpose did you bring me here if not to *save* him?"

There was no reply, no explanation. There was only Iviana crying before the body of an innocent man. She had no idea why this had been done or why she had been brought to see it. *How could my Great Friend be so cruel?* she asked. She thought she knew Him well, thought she was beginning to understand His ways, and now she knew nothing at all.

The sounds of the Anointed One's body being lowered to the ground caught Iviana's attention and her once bound feet moved swiftly toward them. Those few who cared for him sobbed as they removed the spikes from his body. Yet unseen, Iviana knelt beside his face and gazed on it, at last drawing her hand up and placing it upon his cheek. It startled her to discover it was warm, as if life might still pulse within it, but it could not be. This powerful man, whoever he had been to these others who felt as she did, was gone.

Iviana had come, she had witnessed his murder, but had been unable to do anything for him. Her hand still on the raw flesh of his cheek, she turned away and whispered, "Please...please...take me back to my friends."

At once, a bright light seared across her vision and in the next moment she was beside the lake.

Madly, Iviana raced back to the campsite. On her way, she noticed the sun breaking through the dark sky. As she tripped over a tree stump and into the camp, she sobbed still. Sitting up where she fell, she rocked herself as tears continued to fall. She wondered how the Great One could have let her see what she had seen. It was cruel and she couldn't fathom how it could not be so. Her Great Friend had revealed a side she had not expected. He had allowed that man to die in the cruelest way and had brought her to watch it.

Those who were in the camp awoke and rushed to where they heard her sobbing, Nimua in the lead. "Ivi, what is the matter?" she cried, kneeling beside her friend. "What has happened to you?"

Iviana tried to speak, but her voice was gone from

her previous screaming. Nimua tried to take hold of her hand, but Iviana batted it away in frustration. She drew her knees to her chest and hugged her arms around them, concealing her sobbing face within them.

Brenna placed her hand on Iviana's back, but her anger was yet fresh and she nudged the girl's hand from her. Iviana could not understand her own emotions or why she was reacting to her friends in this way. She only knew she felt so very raw and vulnerable. Since she'd become friends with the Great One, she'd always felt He was looking out for her. Now that she had watched that man's violent death, had seen him abandoned to the fate that dark creature had conjured, her certainty wavered and it frightened her. She felt vulnerable in a way she hadn't since her mentor passed away.

Flynn attempted to come near her as well, but stopped himself, fearing he would make it worse. Marquen marched into the woods to intercede for the girl who sat weeping without explanation. Nimua and Brenna only watched, hating there was nothing they could do, while Necoli stood back, knowing full well the last person Iviana wanted to see was him.

Having awoken earlier than the others, Darist had

missed the episode entirely. He entered the camp with a load of wood he had fetched to build a fire for breakfast. Nimua raced to him, explaining what had happened and that Iviana wouldn't allow anyone near her.

Before Nimua could finish, Darist looked to where Iviana wept, dropped the wood he carried and raced to her side with purpose in his heart; he would not be turned away. Quietly, he knelt and wrapped his strong arms around her. At first, Iviana meant to free herself from his unwanted grasp, but found he could easily hold her without much trouble, his Great Gift as aid.

Iviana relented. She turned in his arms and cried against his shoulder. There the two sat for some time until Iviana was worn with crying and fell into a weary sleep.

≈ 9 ∽

HOURS LATER, Iviana awoke to find herself alone in her tent. The sun shone brightly outside, but it did nothing to cheer her. She was utterly worn and raw and could find no reason to move from her bed. Recalling the way she had treated her friends when she entered the camp that morning, she was ashamed of her behavior, but had no desire to offer any explanation of what had happened. She wanted to be alone and knew they would have no better understanding of the occurrence than she. If anything, they would probably assume she had dreamt it, but she knew very well it had not been a dream. It had been only too real for her.

Iviana remained in this attitude for days while her friends awaited direction. She would not speak to anyone—not even the one she had allowed to comfort her. They wondered whether she willfully refused to speak or had simply lost her voice entirely. All they knew was that Iviana was not herself.

One evening while Iviana lay in the tent, she heard the others whispering outside.

"She's been like this for days," Nimua said. "We can't just leave her like this."

"She's tired—perhaps ill," said Marquen, considering. "If you're thinking of getting her back to the Greater Archipelagos, I don't know if she has the strength for such a trip."

"I agree," Darist added thoughtfully. "Whatever happened, she needs time to heal."

"Well, we can't just wait around for something to happen. We need to *do* something," said Nimua.

"I think I may have a solution," offered Flynn. "My sister married a man who owns an estate not far from here. If we can find a way to get her there, she may rest there as long as she likes. I would not at all mind seeing my sister again, either."

"That's perfect," Darist answered, obviously relieved.

"Indeed, it is!" Nimua replied happily. "I think it might do her good and then we can all meet this sister of yours."

"That settles it," said Marquen. "We leave as soon as possible. Tomorrow?"

As the rest offered their agreement, their voices faded as they moved to another area of the camp until Iviana could no longer hear what was said. Her face red with shame, she regretted the situation she had created, yet she did not feel ready to seek, even if that was an option. She was not ready for anything and, try as she might, she could not get herself out of this mindset. Nevertheless, she was determined to try.

The next day, Iviana forced herself out of the tent as soon as she had changed. She was surprised at how weary she felt and was so dizzy she fell against the tent. She caught hold of one of the tent-pegs until she was steady.

"Ivi!" Flynn exclaimed. "What are you doing up? You look utterly white in the face, my friend."

Iviana put on as lively a face as she could manage. "I'm feeling much better, Flynn. I think we might continue our journey today."

"Oh, my darling dragon savior, I am glad you feel up to it, but I've already made other arrangements. We're going to see my sister at her estate."

"Are we?" Iviana asked a little faintly. She was surprised by how woozy she was feeling. She had planned to go against the plan her friends had made, but when he said it that way—as a trip to see his sister—she found it difficult to argue.

Just then, a grand looking carriage pulled into the site.

"What is that?" Iviana asked, baffled.

"This, my dear, is a ride. I went on ahead last night to see my sister and inform her of our coming and I borrowed this little gig. You mind?"

Iviana's plans had been totally thwarted, for the thought of riding in that warm, luxurious carriage was too appealing for her to reject. She surprised herself and allowed Flynn to escort her to it. She even waited while he pulled open the door and helped her in.

"Thank you," Iviana said meaningfully. It felt good to be in a homey, beautiful carriage, rather than sitting or sleeping on the ground and walking on and on through the woods.

"You're perfectly welcome," he told her. "I'll be back in a moment."

On the seat of the carriage was a long shawl. She took this, covered her arms with it and waited, wondering if she was leaving her friends to pack everything without her, but did not worry for long. In a few moments, she was asleep.

The next thing Iviana knew, the carriage had come to a stop before the beautiful estate of her friends Sir Retrom and Flynn's sister who was now called Lady Laurel. In the coach with her was Nimua, who sat beside her, and Darist, Marquen and Brenna, who looked a little squashed on the seat across. She wondered where Flynn and Necoli were until she saw them arrive beside the carriage on horseback. She supposed that made sense, as none of the others would have had any experience riding as there were no horses in the Greater Archipelagos—at least, none she had seen.

It wasn't long before Laurel approached the carriage, her face flushed with joy. Iviana was almost grateful she had caused this side-trip if it meant Flynn could spend time with his sister again. It had been nearly a year since they had seen one another and she remembered how close they had been before she'd dragged Flynn into the Greater Archipelagos as future Realm Leader. Now they were back on the estate, Iviana realized how odd it felt that Flynn was now the official Realm Leader of the Greater Archipelagos, as this was the last place Flynn had been ordinary, old Flynn; she missed him.

The carriage door opened and Iviana met the eyes of the young woman she had not seen for some time. As a large smile spread across Laurel's face, Iviana remembered how close they had been before she had left the realm with Flynn.

"Ivi, it is so wonderful to see you," Laurel said gleefully. She did not sound like the Laurel Iviana had left, but like a refined, young woman. This new Lady Laurel turned to the others who were in the carriage. "Welcome, all of you! I cannot tell you how happy I am to have the privilege of meeting you and I hope we will all become good friends." She cast them all a warm smile and stood aside while the footman helped them out.

When Iviana stepped down, her legs were weak, as if she had run for miles, and she was grateful when Nimua and Brenna attached themselves to each of her arms. Iviana heard Nimua gasp and caught a pleased twinkle in the eyes of the others as the sight of the beautiful castle they were being welcomed into stood tall before them. Truth be told, it was a small castle, as far as castles went, but it was more beautiful and grand than anything in the Greater Archipelagos.

As the group followed Laurel inside, Iviana noticed how the people they passed—mostly servants—stared in confusion. She knew they must be a rare sight: her in her plain, Kierelian clothes fit for a poor man, while the others wore the togas standard to the Greater Archipelagos.

Soon, they were escorted to their rooms. It seemed there was space enough for each to have their own and Iviana was shown into a lovely, comfortable one. As soon as she had a look around at all the finery, she sat herself on the bed and touched her head. It was pounding away at a rapid rate. Oh, what she wouldn't give for some hefesplis, but the plant could not be found in this world.

Iviana jumped when the door to the room suddenly flew open and a plain, little woman entered breathing heavily.

"I'm sorry, miss, if I've startled you. I was supposed to be here to meet you when you came in and have that fire going and a nice, steaming bowl of broth waiting. But you see, while I was waiting for the soup, I took a seat on the cellar stairs and must have drifted, for I did not wake up 'til young Doggins gave me a good hard pat on the back and said I was late in coming. Please, forgive me, miss."

Iviana couldn't help the giggle that escaped her lips, something she had not done for days. The way the woman had burst in all in a tizzy and gone on so quickly with her explanation as though Iviana was some noble made her forget the troubles of the last few days.

"Please, forgive me," Iviana said through her giggling. "Oh, I'm so sorry. Please, don't trouble yourself. I'm not accustomed to being waited on. I'm certainly not at all troubled by your being late."

The maid looked Iviana over, not at all understanding the young woman's fit of giggles, but assumed it was related to her illness. She'd been informed she was not to let the girl out of her sight and to nurse her back to health if she could.

"Well, miss, I thank you for not being sharp with me. I will get that fire going and have a tray brought up for you. You're not expected at dinner, so I may as well help you change too. We'll have you snuggled up in that bed just as soon as we get some heat."

Iviana tried to tell the woman she could start her own fire and could certainly dress herself, but the woman would have none of it. She could see the paleness of the face before her and the dizzy look in her eyes and knew what the girl needed was to be taken care of.

It wasn't long before Iviana found herself dressed in the prettiest nightgown she had ever seen and tucked into the huge, sumptuous bed, being spoon-fed by the maid who sat on a chair beside her.

"What's your name?" Iviana asked between mouthfuls.

"I beg your pardon, miss. I hadn't realized I'd not told you my name. Merlow is what I'm called by my friends or Merlowena by my betters as it's my full name."

"I like Merlow."

A real warmth entered the eyes of the woman at that. "Then that's what I'll answer to if ever you're needing anything, miss."

"Please, call me Ivi."

"Oh, no, miss, I couldn't. If I was caught calling you by a personal name like that, I'd be in for it. Could I call you by your full name, miss? If 'miss' will not do?"

"Of course," Iviana replied easily, but smiled a little by what she was called when the woman spoke again.

"That's the end of the bowl, miss, and I'm glad of it. That's a good start."

"Why was I not expected at dinner?" Iviana suddenly wondered.

"Well, miss," the woman began as though uncertain her reply would be satisfactory. "Because...you haven't been well, miss."

Iviana lay back on her pillow. How she had become as weak as she was, she did not know. She supposed she had taxed herself in the emotional state she'd been in for so many days. Well, she would bring herself to full health soon. She wouldn't laze around and remain a burden.

℘

When Merlow entered the room the following morning, she was caught quite by surprise at the sight of Iviana awake and waiting for her. "I'm sorry, if I've come late, miss," she said as she stoked the fireplace.

"It's quite alright, Merlow," Iviana assured. "I've just decided I'm going to get better."

"Is that so?" the maid asked behind the smile she was attempting to hide. "Well, lets just have a look at you." She stood beside Iviana and peered closely. Iviana was still rather pale, but her spirits were better and that gave her hope the girl would accomplish her goal. "Well, I'll have a nice, big breakfast brought in

159

for you and we'll see how much you can manage to eat."

Iviana was disappointed by how little she was able to consume before she felt she could eat no more. The food held no taste for her and it felt like it sat heavy in her stomach like a soggy log. "This is no good," said Iviana. She thought a moment before, "Merlow, if I made up a list, could you get someone to bring me what I need?"

"Why, yes, of course. What is it you're needing?"

Iviana told her the things she wanted—they were things she would have used for one of her patients—and with each item the eyes of the little servant woman grew larger. "Miss, I think you may be trusting me to get these things for you myself," she said when Iviana had finished.

Iviana would have liked to disagree and save her the trouble, but she understood Merlow's reasons. She and her mentor had been accused of witchcraft too many times for her not to know Merlow's suspicions and that she wished to protect her patient from rumor.

A while after Merlow had gone out—a little against her will since she had been told not to leave Iviana's side—Iviana heard a knock at the door. She was startled by the sound, uncertain as to who it could be, for she was still in her nightgown, her hair unkempt. Merlow had made her promise she would comb through it while the maid was away, but she had not yet done it. Though it was customary to go to the door, she was determined to regain her strength, so she called from her bed to ask who it was.

"My Seeker, it is your Realm Leader, so you may not turn me away," a merry voice called through the door.

Iviana was a little timid about seeing her companions since she hadn't really spoken with them for the past few days. Not to mention the fact she was in a frilly nightdress. Even so, she felt there was no choice but to welcome him.

"Very well!" she called. "Come in, oh, Realm Leader, if you must."

Flynn opened the door and answered with a mock bow while Darist strolled in behind him with a sheepish grin. She supposed he was a little frightened of her because of the way she had behaved while she was in her "state." She would have to be very gracious to make up for it now and show them she was healing.

"I'm so glad you've come," she greeted them warmly. "I was afraid I was going to be kept in solitary until fully active."

Darist looked like she had relieved him of a great burden. "You're sounding much better."

"Don't I *look* any better, then?" asked Iviana with a grin. She truly wanted to seem her old self. "Merlow did seem a little doubtful when she looked me over this morning."

"Who is *Merlow?*" asked Flynn with a glimmer of mischief in his eyes, as if silently accusing her of keeping some great secret from him.

"Merlow is none of your concern," she answered slyly.

"Well, if you intend to keep this Merlow all to yourself, I suppose we cannot *make* you tell us."

"Who's needing me?" the breathless Merlow asked as she entered the room with her secret stash of Iviana's requested things. The woman sat her basket on a table, careful to tuck the blanket over what she'd fetched for Iviana. "I'm sorry I'm late, miss," she said as she caught her breath.

"You're not at all late," Iviana eased. "I wish you wouldn't worry so. I was just telling my friends you looked as though you secretly thought I appeared sickly this morning."

"Oh, my, miss. It isn't that you look sickly—you are a very pretty lass—you only look a little pale is all! I'd not meant to let on."

"It's perfectly alright to tell my friend she looks sickly, Merlow," Flynn eased with his most winning smile. "I think it only honorable to speak truth to one's friend."

As Merlow was not well-acquainted with sarcasm or teasing in general, she turned on him with, "It is not gentlemanly, sir, to speak of this young lady so. Perhaps, you should practice a quiet tongue, like your strong-looking friend over there. And one more thing…are you not aware that young men in the room of a single, young woman without a chaperone could very well ruin her reputation?"

Iviana swallowed a choke, but noticed Flynn was quite humbled.

"Merlow," he said. "You have given me very sound advice, indeed. I will absolutely watch my tongue when I speak of this young lady or any other. As for her reputation, I am afraid I have quite forgotten my manners as I have been in a very distant region. I will brush up on them hereafter, I assure you. My humblest apologies."

Iviana glanced at Darist and they exchanged fairly amused grins.

"Well," Merlow began, feeling rather more merciful after this speech. "See that you do. I will not have to see you out, now, I suppose."

Flynn gave the servant woman a perfectly charming bow that made the little woman blush, as she was not used to such behavior. He followed with, "I thank you, kind woman. I will remain only a little while longer, however, and then I must keep the appointment I have set with Laurel."

Merlow turned on him again, though not so harshly as before. "That's *Lady* Laurel to you, young man."

Iviana watched as Darist took his turn at choking back his laughter, but Flynn didn't miss a beat. "Of course, my good woman. I apologize." He offered her another repentant bow before taking his leave.

Having made his exit, Iviana thought it only right to explain Flynn's situation. "Merlow, I thank you for scolding that roguish man, but I feel I must tell you that he is Lady Laurel's brother. They're very close, so—"

"Oh, good gracious!" the woman exclaimed as her hands flew to her cheeks. "I had no idea he was the Lady's own brother. Oh, dear, I will lose my place—certainly, I will." The woman was entirely flustered and it took some doing for Iviana and Darist to assure her nothing of the kind would happen—that Flynn meant his apology and would not speak of the matter to a soul.

"Now, Darist," Iviana began. "You have to tell me how beautiful the dinner was last night. Are you all enjoying yourselves?"

"Well, I can tell you it's been an adventure. Never have I eaten at such a table or been in as large a place as this. The grounds are stunning. I can see why you left us for your own world—er—land."

Iviana grinned, but her smile faded just a little as she wanted to assure him, "You know, I think the Greater..." She glanced over at Merlow who sat looking over the things she had brought for Ivi. "I think your home is just as beautiful—even more so in some ways."

Darist understood her meaning. "It's just that Kierelia is home, is that it?"

Iviana was uncertain whether or not the statement was correct. "I suppose so. It's what I'm used to anyway. Things with Kurnin and some of the other islanders, even Nico and Leilyn...I just didn't feel as comfortable as I would have liked. I wanted my mentor's home and I wanted to do what I felt the Great One desired. So I left."

"I see," Darist replied. "And how...how are you feeling now?"

Iviana's face clouded, but she answered, "I think I'm better than before and I hope I'll continue to get better."

Darist nodded, but appeared to be wrestling with something.

"What is it?" Iviana asked.

"It's nothing...Well, that is to say, we've been very worried. You don't have to talk about what happened, but I can't help wondering and worrying over it, that's all."

"I'm so sorry, Darist. I'm sorry for being so..."

"Ivi, you don't have to apologize—"

"No, I want to and I wish I could tell you what took place, but I'm still so confused. It would be too hard to explain. I may tell you all one day, but not just now...I *will* tell you that I endured no physical harm."

"Well, I'm grateful to hear that, at least, and I'll tell the others, if you don't mind. I know it isn't much, but as I said, we've all been very worried."

"Oh, please, tell them. I should have said so days ago."

Darist was about to reply when there was another knock at the door.

"I'll answer that, if you don't mind, miss," Merlow informed.

After a few soft words were spoken, a thin, blonde being flashed across the room to where Iviana and Darist were.

"Oh, Ivi, you're looking so much better," Nimua said as she approached. "I'm *so* happy to see you so—oh, that nighty is divine! You look simply endearing in it, doesn't she Darist? Ivi, now, ignore my prattle. How are you doing?"

Iviana smiled affectionately at her friend. "I'm doing much better now someone has looked at me and not seen a sickly face," she told her.

"Now, miss," Merlow interrupted. "I will say you've gained a great deal of color since I last looked at you."

"Oh, yes, Ivi, you really do look like a perfect picture sitting in that beautiful bed just as you are. In fact, I wish I could paint you there. Doesn't she really look like a picture, Darist?"

"Yes," was Darist's reply.

Nimua laughed at him. "Well, don't go on about it, Darist. We don't need a book. Oh, heavens, I forgot! Brenna is waiting outside. She didn't want to come in until she knew she would be welcome. Of course, I don't take heed of such things, generally. When I want to see my friend, I see my friend. Now, just a moment, I'll go fetch her."

As Brenna entered in a lovely pink gown, Iviana realized all her friends were dressed in very fine Kierelian clothing—certainly the clothes of gentility. She, herself, had never worn anything of the sort. At any rate, she was struck by how lovely and sweet Brenna looked in her flowing gown trimmed with lace. There was no question as to why Flynn had been in such high spirits earlier.

For the next hour, the four enjoyed compatible conversation until Merlow insisted they allow Iviana a quiet repose. After days of being alone in a dark tent, Iviana was disappointed to see them go, but knew it would be worth it when they could be on their way again.

&

The rest of that day and the entirety of the next few days were spent on Iviana nursing herself back to health and making good use of the herbs and things Merlow had brought for her. All the while, the little maid looked on as though she really questioned the integrity of Iviana's practices.

One day, she caught Iviana willing the purple glow of her healing through her hand, using the Healer's most precious gift. Iviana now knew the gift had come from the Great One, but poor Merlow had no way of knowing what went on and this had gone too far for her.

Gasping, she spoke with deep concern, "Iviana...n–n–now I've been quiet all these last few days, but I have just got to say now, if it's witchcraft you're dabbling in, I am that worried for your life. I can't agree with these doings myself and what would Sir Retrom do if he caught you at it? Why, he might just turn you in to young King Curiel himself, even if you are such a good friend of the Lady's."

"Oh, Merlow, I'm so terribly sorry for having distressed you," was Iviana's genuine reply. "I'm afraid I would have a time explaining just what it is I do, but I promise you—I give you my word—I would never, ever use witchcraft."

Merlow studied her patient thoughtfully. "Well...I believe you and how glad I am to hear it. I won't ask any more questions; your word is enough. I am a simple woman and the great many things I don't understand, I am perfectly happy not knowing all there is to know about them." She paused a moment before she admitted, "You do look much stronger, at that. I think you might just leave your room tomorrow, if you think it best."

৪০10৩

THE GARDENS ON Sir Retrom's estate were well known throughout Kierelia, for they had been designed by masters in decades past and been meticulously kept since. It was in the very center of this garden Iviana lounged across a bench of wicker, tucked away in a secluded corner where red and white roses towered around her. As the wind blew the buds in merry dance, stray water droplets from a nearby fountain splashed onto her face. She did not mind, however, as she sat reading a book from the castle library; it was refreshing and she was at peace.

Unbeknownst to her, she had been discovered in her hiding place by a well-dressed man. As Iviana sat among the roses, her dark, curling hair pulled back loosely at the nape of her neck and dressed in a Kierelian gown of brilliant red material, the man was captivated by the sight of her reading form and, seeing her clothing—a loan from Laurel—assumed she was of some status, as was he. He strove to think up some excuse to speak with the beauty on the bench, but concluding he had none, made his way to her without one. When she was so absorbed in her story she did not notice his approach, the man rubbed the back of his neck, searching for his next words.

"What is it you read there, my lady?" he finally muttered.

Iviana yelped in surprise at the stranger's sudden appearance. "I'm sorry," she replied breathlessly. "I didn't know anyone was nearby."

"No, the fault is mine!" cried the man, secretly scolding himself for his stupidity. "I'm terribly sorry I startled you." An idea entered into his mind and he added, "Please, allow me to make amends by showing you about the property. I am good friends with Sir Retrom and know it well. But then, perhaps you do as well and I have made my offer in vain."

Iviana was speechless, for, now she had a chance to study the stranger, it was apparent he was a man of some rank; she had never in her life spoken to one of these before, aside from Sir Retrom; but Sir Retrom had a way of making himself accessible to anyone.

"Er—thank you, sir. I'm not very familiar with

the grounds, but I have promised not to move from this spot until one of my friends come to claim me. I haven't been well, you see, and I'm still recuperating."

"Ah, then you are on the mend if you are out of doors. I'm glad of it. Will you be well enough to attend the forthcoming festivities?" he asked hopefully.

"Festivities? I don't know what you mean?"

"I am surprised to hear that. There is to be a ball. That is why I am here; I like to arrive early to mingle with the other early arrivals. If you don't mind my asking, how do you come to be at Sir Retrom's estate and not know about the event?"

Iviana hesitated. She had no idea who this gentleman was nor why he cared at all about her affairs. "I had been traveling when I was taken ill. A friend of mine suggested we come here until I've recovered. We only arrived a few days ago and I suppose no one has wanted to excite me with the news," Iviana finished, but could not help adding, "Sir, may I ask who you are?"

"Forgive me. I have been utterly rude, haven't I? I am Loric, son of the duke of Floresbury," he answered with a bow, taking her hand at the same moment. "And who might you be?"

"Oh..." replied Iviana. *How can this man be speaking to me?* "I'm Iviana."

Loric bowed over the hand he held. "Lovely to make your acquaintance, Iviana." He dropped the hand of the stunned girl. "Would it be impertinent of me to ask you for a dance on the evening of the ball, should you attend?"

Iviana was fairly shocked by his question. She was a poor, little girl of the FairGlenn wood who milked cows, tended garden and healed the sick and wounded. She ought to be no one of consequence to this man, but then, she supposed, he was unaware of that.

"I'm not certain I will be able to attend...but thank you for your kind offer."

Loric awarded her a charming grin before bowing again and saying, "Of course. I pray your health continues to mend and I really do hope to see you on that evening. I fair you well, Iviana." With that, the astonishing gentleman departed.

A long, low whistle sounded from the other side of the roses, startling Iviana.

"Who's there?" she called.

Strutting toward her from the other side of the roses was Darist in very fine Kierelian clothing. Iviana thought if she didn't know better, she would easily mistake him for nobility. Laurel and Sir Retrom had certainly been generous to her and her friends.

"What were you doing eavesdropping on my conversation?" she asked a little sourly as she dropped her legs from the bench so he could sit beside her.

Darist grinned. "I do admit I was eavesdropping, but it wasn't my intention to begin with. I only came to take you inside. Nimua wants you for another chess match. Anyway, I came in at the end of your conversation and didn't want to intrude on your winning a new suitor."

Iviana glared at him. "I see...Well, I don't like chess. I'm terrible at it."

"I know. And it's too bad, for it's a popular Kierelian game, so I'm told. I am also told the man you were just speaking with is sixth in line for the throne. I have, however, been further informed that that is not as close to the kingship as it sounds, so it is really not so very grand. Still, you've acquired a rather lofty beau, fair maiden."

Iviana blushed, but attempted to cover it with a roll of her eyes. "He is no beau of mine as you are well aware, *Darist*. I've only just met him and have no intention of speaking to him ever again. Really, I can't imagine why he should waste his time talking to me—Wait. Since when do you use words like 'maiden' in passing?"

"When I was taught the word yesterday. I'm trying to broaden my Kierelian vocabulary—but then what do you call his asking you for a dance?"

"I'm glad to hear it, but don't let it grow broader than mine or I shall loathe you—and I don't know what I call it. I *don't* know him is all I *do* know," she replied a little icily.

Darist raised his hands in surrender. "I forfeit! But did you really think Nico would be the only man to ever fall for you? Because you may have to rethink that. Now, before you get cross with me again, shall I take you in to Nimua?"

Iviana groaned. "I suppose...but I'm surely going to lose."

&

Cloaked in nightdress and robe, Iviana sat before the fireplace later that evening when Laurel let herself in. The old friend had been to see Iviana a few of times along with either Flynn or Brenna, but this was the first chance they had to speak privately.

"I see Merlow didn't exaggerate," said Laurel as

she took the chair beside Iviana. "You do look much better. Your eyes look bluer even. How are you feeling, though?"

"I'm feeling a good deal better," was Iviana's reply before changing the subject to something that *wasn't* about her health. "How have you been since you became a fine lady? You look gorgeously regal."

Laurel blushed. "Well, I'm still me, just a little older...and I suppose a little wealthier, if I must admit. I was nervous at first, to help in running the estate, but Retrom and the servants—oh, I feel so silly calling them that—they've been so helpful. It really hasn't been as difficult as I would have thought. I'll admit, on occasion, there are those of rank or even no rank who will snub me because of what I was before, but really, most are very kind. Even the king and queen treated me as almost an equal when I met them. Can you believe that?"

Iviana chuckled. "I really wouldn't know. Closest thing I've ever been to someone of 'status' is our rascally Realm Leader and that's quite different, of course."

"I admit that's what I came to talk to you about. I know Flynn says you haven't been in the Greater Archipelagos much, but how would you say he's doing? He has so much responsibility—more so than

177

any king. I have been so worried about him, imagining him trying to manage an entire planet."

Iviana considered a moment. She had tried not to think of the matter so plainly. Not because she did not believe Flynn was capable, but because she was afraid of how it would affect him. She was afraid he would change too much or the stress would be too great a strain for him.

"Well, he shares a great deal of his obligations with the Island Leaders and the council. Trust me when I say very little gets done without their input and volunteered 'help.' Of course, some of them are truly helpful. Nimua's mother, Naii, is leader of the capital island and I'm certain she'll help him in any way she can."

Laurel released a long breath. "I'm glad I asked you. I knew if there was anything wrong, Flynn wouldn't want to burden me with it.'"

"Well, I will say he seems to be alright so far. Though, keep in mind he's only officially been Realm Leader for a short while."

"Of course," Laurel replied. "Oh, but you will keep an eye on him, won't you? And tell me if he needs anything?"

"Absolutely," Iviana assured. Then wondered if the sudden thoughtful expression on Laurel's face had anything to do with the thought that had just entered her mind.

Their eyes met at the same moment and they read each other's thoughts.

"What of that sweet Brenna?" Leilyn asked her a little quietly. "She seems very kind and brave, from what I hear."

"Oh, she is. I don't know her as well as I'd like, but she's more than just a lovely face. She has rare qualities."

"I gathered as much," Laurel replied happily. "Do you think—"

Iviana nodded. "It's a guess anyway."

"Well, you will keep me informed?"

"Of course, but I should think you would know before me."

"Mmm, but you are his dearest friend, I think," Laurel admitted. "We'll see what happens. To be honest, I used to think he felt that way about you, but I suppose I was wrong...Speaking of, I heard you met Loric today?"

Iviana was surprised. "You did? How? Did Darist—"

"Loric told me. He's one of Retrom's best friends, you know."

Iviana raised a brow. She knew where Laurel's

thoughts were. "Is he, now?"

"Mhm. He spoke highly of you."

"Good."

"Oh, Ivi, admit you're flattered! Do you know who he is? He's the king's favorite nephew and heir to the throne!"

"*Sixth* in line from what I hear and apparently that's not so very grand. And why should that matter to me? It doesn't impress me...at least not in any way that would make me *like* him."

"Well, if that doesn't do it, perhaps you noticed his looks? He's a very sought after man, Iviana."

"Laurel! Tell me you didn't marry your Retrom for money or looks! I know you better than that."

Laurel huffed at her through a smile. "Goodness, you're as stubborn as the day I met you."

"Of course, I am. I'm friends with your brother; I have to be or he'd win every argument."

Laurel laughed. "That is surely reason enough."

∞

The next morning was cool and more than fine enough for Iviana to join Nimua, Laurel and Brenna for a lounge in the brilliant garden again. All about them was a magnificent spectacle of colorful flowers, shooting fountains and graceful statues. Iviana leaned back on the grass beneath her and breathed deeply of the perfumed air. Beside her was Laurel, watching with amusement. Nimua and Brenna were set on a wooden bench before them.

Iviana sat up suddenly and exclaimed, "Nimua, tell me how you like Kaern!"

Nimua and Brenna looked at her with glittering eyes as Nimua replied, "It's beautiful. We've nothing like this sort of scenery in the Greater Archipelagos...and your clothing," she looked down at the long, flowing Kierelian gown she wore, "is so delicate and grand. I love it."

"Not everyone's is," Iviana explained. "You've seen how I dress."

When she had dressed in her own clothing the morning before, Merlow had frowned and left the room to return with an exquisite gown fit to be seen by the upper classes housed in the castle.

"I know," said Nimua. "I thought everyone in Kierelia dressed like you...not that you dress poorly or anything."

Iviana laughed. "Of course I do. I dress like a man."

Nimua nodded a little against her will. "I *had*

noticed. Perhaps more like the men who clean the stables."

"Iviana dresses for practicality," Laurel defended.

Iviana turned to Brenna. "And what do you think of this land?"

Brenna's eyes lighted again. "I love it. It smells like a dream...at least it does in this garden. Your stables smell...less like a dream. Though, I love those horse-creatures. They look somewhat similar to dragons. Flynn has promised to take me riding one of these days."

"Well, you're a lucky girl. I've never ridden myself," replied Iviana.

"Have you ever danced?" Laurel asked her.

"I don't know that I've attempted anything more than a spin in my life."

It was quiet a moment and Iviana knew what they were thinking about, but waited for them to speak.

Finally, Nimua said tentatively, "Ivi, we want to ask you something."

Iviana looked over the three young women and wondered what they were after. "Alright..."

"We were wondering if...you had any idea of when we will be moving on? You see, there is this...this affair that Laurel and Sir Retrom are hosting—it's called a ball—that's just around the corner and we were so hoping it would work out for us to remain for it. Besides...I hear you've already been asked to save a dance for a certain someone...a certain eligible someone."

Iviana wasn't certain how to answer. She knew, no matter what had happened, she had a mission to complete. She was supposed to be leading her friends to wherever this glowing parchment was, but she still felt raw and uncertain. It had been such a struggle to get this far and yet she felt no direction from the Seeker's gift. She wondered if she'd missed something, but knew very well she hadn't. When it came right down to it, she was lost.

"I've never been to a ball—only heard little things." She was quiet a while longer, fiddling with the grass at her feet. She continued with sudden decision, "We will be here, you can depend on it. I don't think it would be any trouble if we were to leave after that time, if Flynn thinks he can be spared longer from his duties, that is. Really, you should be asking him."

"Oh, we have," Laurel replied. "He says he would love to go so long as you say it's alright."

"Then plan on attending your first ball, ladies. It will be my first as well. Though I will *not* be dancing, no matter *who* asks me to."

"Oh, *Iviana!*" cried Nimua. "Are you going to run from every boy who likes you? I've heard wonderful things about this one and I think you should give him a chance. Why, we can remain here in Kierelia as long as you like if you need time to get to know him better."

Iviana surprised herself as she considered this. Was everyone right? Was this Sir Loric interested in her and should she return his interest? Perhaps she was writing him off too quickly. But this sort of thinking was foreign to her.

Nimua, Laurel, and Brenna began to make plans for what they would wear to the ball, but Iviana continued her own thoughts, fiddling with the blades of grass beside her. She had been beginning to gain some measure of peace, but it was slightly marred now she had asked herself these questions—not only because getting married had been the last thing on her mind for as long as she could remember, but because she was yet uncertain she had made the right decision about remaining any longer than they already had.

If she was to remain at the castle in an attempt to get to know this man, it would further prolong the quest. What if she truly was supposed to find the parchment and its message was as imminent as

Rhimesh had made it sound? What if this quest had a time limit? All the same, the decision to remain until the ball was over had been made. Besides, she did not feel she was in any position to try seeking again.

As she pondered these things, Iviana heard faint laughter somewhere behind her and assumed it was someone passing—perhaps a gardener. Now, as she felt rather than saw a black shadow looming behind her, she really wondered what could possibly be there that the others, who had a better view than her, had not noticed.

Iviana slowly turned, but as quickly as she glimpsed a faintly lucid being, there appeared to be nothing at all. She stood and looked around as far as her eyes could see, but there truly was nothing to be seen but a fair-weather day. *I wonder if I should have left my sick-bed after all*, she wondered dizzily.

Iviana excused herself to her room, but was followed shortly by Nimua, who was not remiss in watching for the slightest sign of relapse in her beloved friend. Shrugging off all questions and concern, Iviana relented to Nimua's staying with her while she rested, but she did not plan to share the occurrence.

"I feel I've hardly seen you since we've been here," said Iviana. "Precisely what has been occupying your time?"

Nimua looked up nonchalantly and replied, "I've been so busy with Necoli teaching me how to dance that these few days have felt like a breath. I hadn't realized just how quickly the time was passing."

"You've been learning to dance?" asked Iviana, impressed. "How does Necoli know how to dance?"

"I don't know. He says he picked it up in his travels. He's really very good at it. You'd be surprised at how graceful he can be. Necoli looks very different when dressed in elegant clothing, too. Anyway, he says my dancing is looking perfectly effortless now and I certainly hope so since we've been practicing several times daily."

"You like him," Iviana ventured.

Nimua looked away. "Of course. He's very nice."

"You like him more than that..."

"Oh, Ivi, you don't blame me, do you?" Nimua asked fearfully

"Of course I don't blame you!"

Nimua released a long breath. "Oh, thank heaven. I have wanted to tell you since the moment I realized it, but I was afraid you would think it unfair to Darist and you two have been so chummy lately."

"It will only be unfair if you don't tell him. Otherwise, you can't help it, I suppose." Iviana hesitated a moment before adding, "Do you think these feelings...are wise? We don't know him well and he hasn't exactly been eager to share."

"I know he comes off as a bit of a scoundrel," Nimua replied thoughtfully, "but there are moments you can see something...really worthwhile. I think his attitude is only a front."

"I hope so," Iviana replied, nervous for her friend.

"Don't be afraid for me, Ivi. I won't let on how I feel about him. He doesn't need to know...for now, anyway."

Iviana was satisfied with this before something occurred to her. "What about Darist? Do you still have feelings for him?"

Nimua frowned. "No, I don't and I'm so afraid to tell him, Ivi. He'll be so angry!"

"He won't be angry," Iviana consoled. "He'll be upset, of course, but he should be grateful you were honest with him."

Nimua shook her head. "It makes me ill thinking about telling him."

Iviana took her friend's hand. "Nimua, it won't be the end of world. He'll manage and if he is as good a man as I think him, he won't be unkind."

This proved true when, some days later, Nimua

sought Iviana again and exclaimed, "I'm so grateful you urged me to speak with Darist."

"What do you mean? You've told him?"

"Yes, and I'm utterly surprised to inform you he was nearly relieved."

"Relieved?"

Nimua nodded. "I simply told him how it was and I caught him *grinning*. Then he admitted he was glad I had been honest with him. And, you know, he really meant it. We parted friends, just as we've always been."

"Of course you parted friends. Darist is one of the friendliest men to have lived."

"*I know*. But he and I have been friends for so long, I was afraid to lose that. Oh, but it feels so good to have it behind me now."

Iviana embraced her friend. "Now, tell me how your dance lessons with Necoli have been going."

Nimua informed her that Flynn and Brenna had begun to join the lessons. With the four of them ready for the ball, Iviana wondered if she would be able to attend. There was no question about dancing. She simply would not be able to.

❧ 11 ❧

SOME EVENINGS LATER, Iviana joined her friends in the fun they had been having when she had often requested to be left alone to rest. This evening, they were playing games in one of the smaller, cozy libraries and toasting bread on sticks before the fireplace. With a happy heart, Iviana watched as her companions talked and laughed together. It had been some time since she had been able to enjoy the company of all her dearest friends at once. After she had returned from the death of the Anointed One, she simply had not been herself. She hoped she was beginning to return to her former self, even if she was yet sensitive about what she had witnessed that day.

Marquen drew up beside Iviana and cast her a thoughtful smile. "How are you this evening?" he asked.

"I'm well. Happy to be here with you all. I'm sorry to have worried everyone."

"Iviana, it's apparent you've experienced something that has affected you greatly. Though we don't yet know what occurred that night, we're more than happy to forgive you for being a little human in the midst of your troubles."

Iviana relaxed. "Thank you, Marquen," she replied. "Tell me, how have you been enjoying your stay in my home world?" She loved asking this question of her friends, for not long ago she had been in their shoes in the Greater Archipelagos.

"*Is* this your world?"

"Well...no, I don't usually spend my days in such opulence—my home is far simpler than this."

"What I mean is, are you certain this world, this Kaern, is *your* world."

I don't know, Marquen. I don't know where I belong."

"Of course, you do," he answered easily. "You belong with the Great One. Wherever He moves, you should be there."

Iviana struggled with this. She was still so confused.

"Is there anything you need to talk about, Ivi?" he asked.

"Yes...I probably *should* talk about it." She looked about the happy room. "But I don't think now is the time."

"Of course. However, do you mind my asking what we're doing in this fine place? Wasn't our mission, when we set out, to find the parchment that contains the heart of the Great One? We have loitered here for some time."

Iviana sighed. "You're right. Please, just give me time. What happened to me that night has perplexed me. I need to sort some things out."

Marquen nodded. "I understand. I have prayed for you. He has urged me to be patient. So...you have time."

Iviana was surprised by his words. She had not known the Great One approved of her putting off her quest and it baffled her all the more. "I would have thought He'd be upset with me for wasting so much time."

"Sometimes the journey we must take looks much different than we think it should...Now, I see someone is coming to speak with you and I don't want to preoccupy your mind with anything but the joy you see before you. I will leave you." He gave her hand a reassuring squeeze before offering Darist a pat on the back as he approached.

Iviana looked after Marquen and thought how odd it was to see him not only in this setting, but anywhere but his hill. She wondered if he would return to his hermitage after this journey was complete. She couldn't help hoping he wouldn't. It was enjoyable having him around.

"What was that about?" Darist asked, taking the seat beside her. "You looked upset."

"Oh, not upset—maybe a little confused."

"I see. Well, I just wanted to make sure you were alright."

Iviana smiled warmly, saying, "I don't understand why you're so nice to me."

"Neither do I."

"Ah!" She gave his arm a good punch.

Darist laughed and rubbed where she'd hit him. "Alright, that's not true."

The two sat quietly for a while. Iviana was glad silence wasn't awkward between them. They really hadn't known each other all that long, but Darist had always been a comfortable person to be with and she trusted him. For whatever reason, she knew he always thought the best of her and would always defend her. She had known this was true even when she had only just met him. The way he talked to her back then made her feel welcome, as if she belonged—at least when she was with him and Nimua.

"The truth is," he said, startling her from her thoughts, "ever since I first met you, I felt...I don't know...drawn to you."

Iviana stared at the floor. Was Darist trying to say he had feelings for her?

Darist read her face and added with some embarrassment, "Not like that."

Iviana smiled. *Thank the Great One.*

"Don't look so relieved," he added with a grin of his own.

"Sorry."

Darist continued, "I guess I feel more like a brother to you than anything else. The best way to describe it is, when I met you, you felt like my long lost sister or something."

"You know that's not possible, right?"

Darist laughed. "Yes. I do. What I mean to say is..." he couldn't seem to find the words.

"You have my back," Iviana supplied.

He gave her his dimpled grin. "Yes."

"Well, that's good to know."

Darist stood to his feet and offered her a hand up. "Good."

ε᛫

Iviana did not see her friends again until the following evening—the evening before the much anticipated ball was to take place. Finally having regained most of her strength, she had been urged by Laurel, Nimua and Brenna to attend the feast that night. It would be the first time she had done so and she was a little nervous.

When Iviana entered the feasting room, she was struck not only by how grand and festive it was, but also by the great length of the banqueting table. Laurel had informed her that many of the guests who had traveled from faraway places were going to stay on the estate for a few days. Iviana had never seen so many grand people in her life.

When Merlow had dressed her in an exquisite silver gown with long, flowing skirt and delicate lace sleeves, Iviana had begged to be dressed in something else.

"I won't be *comfortable* in a dress like this and I'm nervous as it is," she had told the serving woman.

Merlow replied, "All the same, it's what Lady Laurel had made for you and you look lovely. Now, sit quiet and lets see what can be done with your hair."

When the older woman had finished pulling and prodding at Iviana's dark locks, the younger peered into the mirror. The little maid had not done anything too elaborate in this, at least. Though it was tied at the nape of her neck as she usually preferred, portions of hair on each side of her head had been twisted back until they were fastened into the tail and then woven around the perfect coils Merlow had created.

"Well, your royal highness," Merlow had said when it was obvious Iviana liked it, "will it do?"

Iviana hugged the woman. "Thank you, Merlow."

Now, as Iviana stood in the grand room, she was extremely grateful to Laurel for having had the fine gown made for her. Without it, she would have stuck out like a sore thumb in the midst of the extravagant assemblage.

As Iviana made her way through the crowds, she searched for a familiar face, but the room was extremely full. Once, she thought she spotted Nimua in the midst of a large crowd that seemed enraptured by a blonde who Iviana had mistaken for her. Iviana watched the popular blonde woman charm the large group surrounding and wondered who she was. *She looks as if she could be a princess,* she thought.

Casting her attention to the rest of the room, Iviana marveled at the king's obvious generosity. For the whole of her stay, she had been pondering this. Sir Retrom's estate was beautiful and far more than any mere knight could have ever dreamed of owning if he did not come from a wealthy family. And, though Retrom had been of average wealth, he had not been considered wealthy. Nevertheless, at some point the man had become a dear friend of the king's son, Prince Lancaster, and risked his own life on several occasions for his safety. The castle, a large fortune as well as the opportunity to oversee a few of the nearby villages had been Sir Retrom's reward. For going above and beyond his duty, the king had retired him as a man of great wealth and status. Iviana did not know much about King Curiel, but she was happy to know this.

Suddenly, Laurel was at her side and showing her to the seat she had assigned for her.

"I'm so happy you came. You look lovely in that gown. Merlow told me you asked to not wear it, but I'm glad you did. Anyway, I hope you don't mind not sitting with most of your friends, but Sir Retrom and I like to mix the company so everyone is forced to meet new people. Then, perhaps all will be able to find familiar faces among the crowd at the ball. I did, however, manage to sit you beside that Necoli your friend is always spending her time with. He does seem a nice fellow, doesn't he?" Iviana would have liked to disagree, but Laurel left her to welcome a few others who had just entered the room.

Feeling rather out of place, Iviana tried harder to spot anyone she might know, but before she'd realized it, Necoli was at her side.

"I'm told we're to sit together," he said congenially. "This should be a pleasant evening, don't you think?"

Iviana noticed his manner had changed a great deal since last they had spoken. "Yes, I think it will be," she answered pleasantly.

When at last all guests were seated, Iviana realized, indeed, none of her crew but Necoli was anywhere remotely close. She was disappointed, but decided the food would have to be entertainment enough. Even so, it soon became apparent the mysterious Necoli had endured a great deal of change and was quite open with her.

"I'm happy to see you looking so much better," he said, breaking the silence between them during the second course. "I know we haven't known one another very long, but you did seem so miserable."

Iviana blushed. "I'm not normally like that. I am beginning to feel more like myself."

"Your friends have certainly noticed. They care for you a lot, you know. I don't know that I've ever seen so much compassion among friends in my life."

His words warmed Iviana. "They are gems," she agreed.

By the fourth course, Iviana was pleased that Necoli, who had formerly been so mysterious and false, freely opened up to her.

"You're a Healer, eh?" he was saying in a soft voice as it would not do for anyone to hear this part of the conversation and become curious about their topic. "I grew up among Healers, you know. My parents were missionary Healers."

"Missionary Healers? I've never heard of those."

"Haven't you? They travel all over Kaern, though mostly in Kierelia, using their healing on the ill since the people of this world don't have Healers of their own. That's how I came to know Kierelia. I lived most my life here, traveling with my parents."

"Are you a Healer too, then?"

"No, I'm not and I'm not afraid to admit I'm a little glad of it. I think it would be too much responsibility for me. No, I'm a Swimmer."

"Are You?" asked Iviana, pleasantly surprised. She had been blessed with sharing in the Swimmers' gift of being able to breathe underwater, as Swimmers are able to pass on their gift for a time to anyone they're touching. "I didn't realize. You must love it."

Necoli hesitated. "I suppose so. It does come in handy sometimes and I suppose it is a helpful gift to possess if you live most your life in the Greater Archipelagos, but my parents didn't think it much use to their work. Since we have always traveled in this world, it wasn't often I was able to use it."

"I see. I suppose it wouldn't do for anyone here to learn of such an ability."

"Exactly. At any rate, I wasn't of much use to my parents. I suppose that was why I left them."

"Oh." Iviana thought carefully over the wording of her next question. "Was it difficult to leave them?"

"Not at first. You see, there came a point when my parents and I were no longer seeing eye to eye...I had been getting into mischief wherever we went. I was feeling lost at the time. Anyway, at first the freedom of being apart from them was nice. I got in with a group of pirates and turned my back on the Great One.

"After a time, that life grew taxing. It was against every moral I had been raised with and it wasn't who I was meant to be. So, I left that life. I returned to the Greater Archipelagos and wandered around for a while, attempting to find some meaning—a place I belonged."

"I know that feeling. Did you find a place to settle down then?"

Necoli shrugged. "Nah."

"Oh..." Iviana really felt for the man and regretted her former feeling toward him. She could easily see what Nimua had been talking about.

"Eh, as you said, you've been there. Anyway, a few months ago, I started asking after any word of my parents. I heard they had returned to the Greater Archipelagos, but that was all I could gather. Apart from that, they seemed to have dropped off the face of the planet.

"Finally, I met a friend of theirs who told me their last known whereabouts had been to a newly discovered island that was rumored to contain savages. Most didn't believe the island existed as the explorer who discovered it fell ill upon returning and was unable to lead anyone there before he died. For whatever reason, our council refuses to look into it even though the man gave clues as to its location. At any rate, I thought it made perfect sense that my parents, of all people, would be the first to go and try to work with the savages."

Iviana was struck with a thought. "You're not talking about..."

Necoli nodded sourly. "That's why you found me on the cannibal island. That was the last place my parents tried to use their gifts for the good of others."

"Oh, Necoli..." Iviana thought she would cry. She had been so caught up in her own affairs, she had not been aware of the plight of others. "I had no idea...I can't tell you how sorry I am."

His eyes were very cloudy, then. "I know. I'm sorry too. I wish I'd been with them. They knew nothing about protecting themselves. They were too peaceful. I might have helped."

"Oh, but Necoli, when I met you they had been ready to kill you. too...or marry you off. You can't blame yourself for what you might have done."

"I admit you may be right in that, but when I left them, I left without saying goodbye...without even a note. I wanted to find a place I belonged and now I don't even have them."

Iviana pushed the food around on her plate. There was no way she could eat it.

"Necoli," Iviana began, "I hope you will

continue to travel with us after we leave here." It was all she could think to offer.

The eyes of the man lit up and she caught him unconsciously glance in Nimua's direction. "I would be pleased to."

Through the rest of the meal, Iviana tried to enjoy the entertainment that was offered. The music was truly beautiful and she thought the comedic acts might have been funny had the mystery of Necoli not just been revealed to her. Iviana was kicking herself for the attitude she had had toward him. But Necoli realized he'd just dimmed her first banquet, so worked to lift her spirits.

Near the close of the meal, many toasts were offered up to the host and hostess and to various guests around the table. The popular blonde woman Iviana had noticed earlier received many of these and Laurel stood to offer her brother a heartfelt toast. The room was moved and surprised by the appearance of this brother whom they had not known existed. Iviana noticed he was a little teary-eyed. She thought it must be hard to be away from his only family; she knew better than anyone how much Laurel meant to him. It was wonderful to have seen his joy in the days they had been in her home.

Iviana felt a tug at her arm and a familiar voice

told her she was very sorry, miss, but she needed to speak with her in private. Iviana didn't hesitate to follow Merlow's small form out of the hall. When the two had hidden themselves away in a vacant room, Iviana turned to Merlow, who looked as though she had been crying. "What is it?" she asked the woman who had grown very dear to her over the last few of weeks.

"Oh, Iviana, it's young Doggins," the little maid spoke through her tears. "He's been taken quite ill and it's looking as if he won't make it through the night. The boy is a bit rough around the edges and he's certainly not important, but he's like family to me. I thought, if there was anything you could do, if you cared to, that maybe you could help the lad?"

"Take me to him," Iviana replied.

Merlow led her through a series of hallways and more staircases than she could count until they entered a dark room where a young woman knelt crying beside the bed of the sick young man. Iviana drew near "young Doggins" to examine him. He was unconscious and this worried her. She laid her hand on him and looked for what was draining his life using her Healer's eye.

"Ah," Iviana uttered as she recognized the illness. She had seen this sort of thing before and believed she knew what to do, but she had to get away from the younger woman on the floor before she could say anything. It wouldn't do for Retrom and Laurel to take her into their home and then be accused of housing a witch. Oh, how Iviana wished she could make the people of Kierelia understand as they did in the Greater Archipelagos. She knew by healing the man tonight, she was taking a risk.

Iviana pulled Merlow from the room.

"Now," Iviana began. "I believe I can help him, but we must be as sly as foxes. If anyone were to suspect I had anything to do with his getting well...there would be a good deal of trouble. I'm going to return to my bedroom now. Then, if you can get hold of a few things for me, you can come and fetch me once everyone has gone to sleep and I will do what I can for him. Is that alright with you? I simply don't want to be connected with his healing should he get well. I'm even a little afraid of that girl having seen me."

"Oh, I'm so sorry I didn't think of asking her to do some chore to get her out of the way while you were here. I'll be as sly as a fox *and* wily as a snake from here on out, I promise you."

"I know you will," Iviana replied softly.

When Iviana returned to young Doggins, it was

very late, but as she had anticipated, the halls of the castle even in the servants' quarters were empty. Merlow had retrieved everything Iviana had asked for, but after having applied the treatment to the sick, young man, Iviana found she was having trouble getting herself to use the most precious part of her healing gift on him.

When she had been ill, she had used all the treatments she knew, but refrained from using this precious part of her gift—the part where she willed the healing to take place. For days she had tried to avoid it until she had finally realized she would have to do it if she was going to get well. The trouble was, she knew from Whom her power came and she wasn't at all certain of what terms she and the Great One were on. Her absolute trust in Him had been marred by what she had witnessed that day and she was uncomfortable using the power only He could give her.

Nevertheless, Iviana knew she had to do it, despite her concerns. When at last she came to this conclusion, she began to question whether the Great One would supply the healing in this instance because of the doubt in her heart toward Him. Also, she felt she was being disobedient in not seeking the parchment and this, too, was something she had to work through. In the end, she did all she could to dissuade these fears and looked into herself for whatever trust she could find. There, in the deepest part of her heart, she found her intimate love for the Great One yet burning.

Laying her hands upon young Doggins, she willed his body to accept the treatment. Immediately, her attempt was met with the single moment of purple light that had always come before and had not failed her now. Iviana heaved a breath of relief. The Great One had not turned his back on her and she knew now she would not turn her back on Him. She would trust him no matter what she saw with her natural eye; she would trust that He was *good*.

§

When Iviana awoke in young Doggins' corner chair, she was at first bewildered until she recalled having decided to remain until certain he was on the mend. She was further surprised to find Merlow gone, but supposed she had stepped out on some errand.

Iviana was content with what she found in Doggins. Stepping out of the room, she thanked the Great One for sharing His healing power. She knew how much young Doggins meant to her Merlow and was happy she had been able to help.

Iviana traversed various hallways and stairwells in pursuit of her room before she reached the entrance to the kitchens. Stealing a bite of bread, she realized she was terribly lost. But as there appeared to be no one there, it could not be as near dawn as she had supposed. This meant she had time.

After wandering through a series of yet more corridors and stairwells, the Seeker, working without her Seeker's gift, eventually found herself in the upper part of the castle. Iviana knew full well her room would not be found there, but she was closer. She moved quietly now, as there were sure to be people sleeping behind many of the doors she passed. She did not want to be found wandering the castle on the evening young Doggins had been miraculously healed.

Even so, as she rounded the next corner, a jug of water atop a small table escaped her notice and toppled over, each with little grace and a good deal of clatter. The water seeped generously into the nooks and crannies of the floor as Iviana scrambled to soak it up with the skirt of her dress.

Having returned the table to its former glory, the dreaded sound of a door opening sounded loudly within the corridor. Iviana froze and reminded herself that, though she must be careful, there was really nothing to obviously connect her with the overnight recovery of a servant. Even so, her fears were renewed and she desperately searched for an excuse to offer whoever was coming her way.

"Do my eyes deceive me?" said a merry voice. "Could this sleepwalker be the Iviana I met beside the roses the other day?"

Iviana's gaze fixed on Loric, son of the duke, who leaned against a nearby doorway with a glimmer of humor in his eyes. He was perhaps the last person she wanted to meet at this late hour.

"Er...yes. But I'm not sleepwalking."

"Aren't you? Then, pray, explain what you are doing mopping the floor outside my bedroom door at this hour."

Iviana wished she had owned the sleepwalking excuse.

"I was having trouble sleeping...so I decided to try walking the halls. I'm afraid I got lost in the attempt, however, and have made a mess in doing so."

"Ah, I see," replied Loric, uncrossing his arms and taking a few steps toward her. "Well, it so happens I have been having the very same problem...the sleep difficulty, that is."

Iviana nodded, uncertain how to respond. "I...am sorry to hear it."

Loric reached into his room, threw a robe over his bedclothes and closed the door behind him. "Lady Iviana, I have been good friends with Retrom for many years and have visited his home more times than I can count. If you'll permit me, I am certain I would be able to aid in the quest for your misplaced rooms."

Though Iviana would have preferred no one was aware of her midnight excursion, she knew she must consent if she was ever to make it back without revealing herself to anyone beyond Loric. "Thank you, sir." She had certainly gotten herself into an inconvenient situation.

Loric frowned at her reply. "Iviana, I have given you my name and I would not wish us to go on as strangers. In fact, I now offer my friendship, if you will accept it. After all, it would not be fitting for a stranger to escort you through the castle in the middle of the night."

Iviana had left a good deal of her meekness behind after her adventure in the Greater Archipelagos, but she found she could not refuse his offer, even if she wanted to. He simply was not the sort of person one refused. Besides that, everyone seemed to be urging her to give him a chance...Why not on the night she had healed young Doggins? "...Of course."

Loric was content and urged her to tell him any markers that would help locate her room. Thankfully, he immediately knew the room and it wasn't long before they entered a part of the house she recognized.

"Are you enjoying your stay with Sir Retrom and his Lady Laurel?" Loric asked.

"Oh, yes. Laurel is a very dear friend and her husband a gem."

"I'm glad to hear it. They both speak well of you. I hear you are good friends with Lady Laurel's brother, Flynn, who has recently graced us with his presence. You arrived with him, did you not? Do you know, most people did not even know she had a brother."

Iviana was uncertain how to respond, so said nothing.

Her silence spoke something to Loric, however. He peered into her face, attempting to read her. "Are you and our hostess' brother betrothed, then?"

Iviana laughed. "Oh, no. He's only a dear friend—like a brother."

Loric's face lit up. "I see," he said. As they came

in view of Iviana's chamber, he added, "I am glad to hear it."

"Oh..." Iviana muttered, hoping her flushed face was unreadable in the dim light of the hallway. *They were right,* she realized. Was she comfortable with that? Was she interested?

"Well, here we are," said Loric as they stood before the door to her room.

As her eyes fell upon it, Iviana was surprised by how relieved she was to be there, though she was uncertain as to why, and so turned a joyful face on the helpful man before her. "Thank you so much, Loric," she said. "I truly don't know what I would have done without your help. You have been very kind."

The son of the duke, pleased that she was pleased, offered a gallant bow. "And now that I see you are quite recovered from your recent illness, I wonder if you might grant me a turn at the ball tomor—"

Iviana's relief was dashed when she realized what this grand man was about to ask her. She did *not* plan on making a fool of herself by attempting to dance. Fortunately, before he could finish forming his question, a dazed Merlow came flying up to them.

"Oh, miss," she said with a bow, as she realized who the man with Iviana was. "Forgive me. I have been so worried! I couldn't find you anywhere."

Iviana hoped the woman would be careful not to reveal anything. "Oh, I'm sorry to have troubled you."

Merlow understood she must be careful and settled herself. "No, miss, you haven't been a trouble," she spoke in a humble tone, for Loric's benefit.

Iviana turned to Loric. "Thanks again for helping me."

The man bowed one last time and offered her a meaningful, "Goodnight," before retreating.

When Iviana and Merlow were within the safety of Iviana's room, the little woman immediately started in with, "Oh, Iviana, I have been looking everywhere I could think. I was afraid someone had found you in young Doggins' room!"

"I know, I know. It's all my own stupid fault. I was too tired to wait for you and thought I could find my own way, but I got lost and knocked over a table and that's when Loric found me."

Merlow's tone changed entirely. "How long have you and that handsome Loric been on such friendly terms, missy? You've been holding out on me."

"Not at all! I've only spoken with him once before."

"Well, he is certainly smitten. I think you may be safely married to the sixth heir before long."

"Merlow!" Iviana cried. "I hardly know the man. Besides, I highly doubt he'd truly consider marrying someone of my class."

"I think you must be wrong, my dear," replied Merlow. "What I saw in his face was *intention* and I'll add you'd be a fool not to encourage him."

As Iviana lay in bed, tossing and turning in the early hours of the morning, she truly wished she could be interested in Loric, son of the duke of Floresbury. He certainly seemed nice enough and wasn't at all bad looking or lacking is charm. But when it came right down to it, she felt nothing for him...at least not yet.

∞12∞

AFTER A FEW hours shut-eye before the sounds of the castle made it impossible to sleep any longer, Iviana had awoken with a small stomachache produced by her anxiety over having to attend the ball that evening. She was a simple girl of the woods who lived off the land; she didn't dress in fine clothes nor twirl around dance floors and she had never planned on doing so.

The life she lived in the FairGlenn wood before her mentor passed away had been far simpler than the one she led now, zipping around on the back of a dragon in an attempt to find some magical, glowing parchment and contemplating suitors who expected her to *dance*. She found herself missing her old life. There had never been any pressure to attend social events...especially since she had been an outcast. Now she was not an outcast and should be grateful to attend this affair, but all she could do was worry.

She dreaded being surrounded with all sorts of grand strangers and was well aware she didn't know the proper way to act. On top of that, she would have to be dressed as she had never been before. But, mostly, there would be dancing and she had never learned the art. She hoped and supposed no one would ask her, but there was always the chance Loric would find her.

"Alright, missy. I'll be needing you to sit up if I'm to dry your hair," said Merlow. "Unless you'd prefer your bed soak it up."

Iviana unhappily sat up and allowed the woman to apply a towel to her hair. This was one step closer to the ball. She held her stomach as it groaned.

"Merlow," she began hopefully. "I don't suppose anyone would notice if I decided to remain in my room tonight and gain further rest."

Merlow stopped her drying. "Why, Iviana, what a little chicken you're turning out to be. I have never heard you make up such a tale before. I know as well as you that you're in perfect health and the last thing you need is more rest."

Iviana blushed as the woman continued her drying. "I know..." she sighed. "But don't you see how terrifying this is for me? I'm not of noble birth nor of wealth nor anything that might have prepared me for an evening such as this. How would *you* feel if you were asked to attend a ball?"

"I'd sew myself up in the finest material I could lay my hands on and dawn upon the ball as if I was royalty and that's the truth. I'd pretend I was thirty years younger, at that. Now, I have caught peeks of these events and I do believe you're making a bigger fuss than you should. All you have to do is walk into the room and enjoy all the nice treats those tables will be filled with and have a wonderful time with your friends. Do you think you can handle that?"

This suggestion did relieve Iviana's nerves. She had to admit she had a weakness for tables covered with delicacies, though she had never been near one before. Perhaps the event would be more enjoyable than she was anticipating. After all, her friends were going to be there—even Marquen. Now she thought about it, of course the evening would be enjoyable. It was quite possibly a once-in-a-lifetime opportunity.

Merlow, with the help of another maid, worked on Iviana's hair for what seemed like hours. Iviana really couldn't imagine why doing one's hair would take so long. When she grew tired of sitting so long, she put herself in the position of the women who were doing the work and scolded herself. When at last she was allowed to stand, her head felt strangely heavy.

"Now, don't you be peeking at yourself until we've got you in the gown," Merlow demanded. "It won't look right until then."

The women helped Iviana into a gown unlike anything she had ever dreamed she would wear. It was made of a filmy white material that Laurel told her was beautiful against her skin. It had a pair of small sleeves that wrapped around her shoulders and was completed with a fitted bodice and full skirt that fell like a cloud until it hit the floor.

Once Iviana was dressed and had stepped into a pair of white slippers, she attempted to look into the glass, but was stopped again by Merlow. "We have a few finishing touches yet." The little maid proceeded to pull an intricate, little box from a drawer. "These are gifts from Lady Laurel. She says it's 'a thank you for everything,' whatever that means." When the box was opened, a dainty golden bracelet and necklace, each with a single drop of pearl, were found within.

Iviana stepped away from the stunning gifts. "She cannot have meant to *give* me these things!" she exclaimed.

Merlow gave her that look that conveyed she was being silly...*again*. "I'm afraid so, missy."

Upon receiving the look from her maid, Iviana silently allowed her to add the jewelry to the ensemble. Iviana turned her wrist and watched as the bracelet glistened in the changing light. *That's lovely*, she admitted.

"*Now...*" said Merlow, "you may look at yourself."

Iviana turned slowly toward the mirror and felt something of the feelings she had felt when she had first been dressed in the garments of the Greater Archipelagos. Admittedly, she was very pleased with her appearance. She looked finer and lovelier than she could have ever imagined. With every movement, the fabric shimmered like sunlight on water and each and every little ringlet pinned to her head was placed just so that it complimented the shape of her face perfectly.

Though her appearance was pleasing, she was struck again with anxiety. She was not comfortable being seen like this and wished Laurel had allowed her to choose a plainer material. A simple brown would certainly have suited her better.

"Now, missy, I'm not going to stand here and wait for you to complain about your appearance.

Yes, you look like a queen, but so will many of the other ladies. If you please, I was told you were to meet your friend Nimua in her chamber. She wants to enter the ballroom with you."

Iviana was relieved to hear she would be entering with a dear friend by her side. Immediately, she raced from her room, but tiptoed back to embrace her little maid-friend and thank her for all the work she had done. Merlow took a kerchief from her pocket and dabbed at her eyes before sending Iviana on her way.

"Ivi, you little dear, you really look a dream," Nimua gushed when she opened her door to Iviana's knocking. "Get in here before someone carries you away. Oh, how did Merlow get all of those beguiling curls piled against your head like that? And that dark curl over your shoulder is such a daring contrast with that dashing white gown. Really, I—"

Iviana could stand the praise no longer. "Nimua, I dare say it is *you* who looks like a vision. That deep red absolutely suits you."

"I *know*. I adore this color. Makes me wish we wore it in the Greater Archipelagos."

Iviana agreed and went to open the door for Brenna who was dressed in a stylish green dress. "Oh, Brenna..." she said. "You look exquisite. Are you coming with us?"

"Of course," was her eager reply. "You think I would walk into that terrifying ordeal on my own?"

"How can you be afraid when such festivities await?" cried Nimua. "Now, promise me you'll have *fun,* you two!" The chastened young women agreed and followed Nimua's confidence out of the room and down the corridor.

⁊

Having never before looked into this extraordinarily large room, the eyes of the three were dazzled by the twinkling lights, the people in their fine costume and the overall beauty of the place. Excitement filled each as their eyes were met with color and movement. The musicians in the back of the room sounded rich and grand in the sizable room and Nimua exclaimed she could hardly wait to dance. Iviana and Brenna admitted they would not have missed the occasion for the world and Iviana almost wished she had taken the time to learn to dance as her friends had, it looked so amusing.

It was evident Nimua's wish was soon to be granted when they were met by Flynn and Necoli, who looked as dashing and genteel as any gentleman in the room.

Sounding a surprised whistle, Flynn turned to Iviana with his ornery smirk. "Who knew the mad savior of dragons and damsels could clean up so nicely?"

Iviana rolled her eyes and watched as Flynn's eyes met Brenna's. There was a warm glow cast on each of them as they looked upon one another and Iviana knew her prior suppositions had been correct.

She turned to say something to Nimua, but her eyes fell upon Necoli instead, who stood looking as if he couldn't catch his breath as he gazed at Nimua, her long hair cascading down her back in shining golden waves. Iviana had been accurate in describing her as a vision, but supposed "angel" would have been a better description. The angel offered the breathless Necoli one of her joyous giggles and informed him he had better ask her to dance. The man nodded and offered her his arm, escorting the celestial vision to the floor.

Iviana's attention returned to Flynn as he informed he would be expecting a dance after he had enjoyed a few with Brenna.

"You will do no such thing," Iviana replied. "I cannot dance and I refuse to make a fool of myself."

Flynn thought he might be able to talk her through a few of the dances, but when Iviana avidly conveyed she did not intend to dance, he ceased persisting.

"Suit yourself, Seeker. I, for one, intend to enjoy myself."

Once her friends departed, Iviana intended to enjoy the table where she viewed stacks of cookies and cakes, but on her way, a young gentleman caught sight of her and immediately bolted after her. Iviana couldn't help noticing and, realizing he would wish to dance with her, swiftly fled in search of the nearest shadowy corner. Instead, she trampled the foot of another gentleman, who assured her he would certainly accept her apology if she would have a dance with him.

"Thank you...er, I may, but I am tired now," she told him and scurried along before he had a chance to claim her for one.

At last, she found the dark corner she sought, but spotted another table of delicacies on the way. She stopped at this one and had time to take only a bite of the dessert when she spotted a set of gentlemen on their way toward her. Attempting to flee, her dress caught on the edge of the table.

"I have not had the pleasure of making your

acquaintance," began one of the men as he arrived at her side.

"Nor have I," put in the other as he arrived breathlessly behind the first, casting an irritable glance at his friend.

The first interrupted with, "I saw you as a sparkling light within this dim room—"

"As did I," agreed the other.

The first took hold of Iviana's hand and asked for her name.

"Iviana," she supplied, nearly choking over it.

"Aah, a beautiful name that well-suits a woman of your divine appearance. I am Ral—"

"Frank," put in the other. "And I would be most appreciative if you would—"

"If you would dance with me," ended the other, bowing over her hand.

This time, Iviana had a reply prepared. "I cannot," she said. The two looked stricken before she ended with, "I am famished and must finish this cake."

"Aah, my ravishing picture of feminine beauty," said the man who had hold of her hand. "I will wait with you until you have finished."

"As will I," added the other.

Iviana had not expected patience.

She removed her hand from the vise that held her. "Will you, indeed?" said she, thinking quickly. She looked about and espied the popular blonde woman from the banquet the evening before. "But you see, you must wait for me here while I take some of this cake to my friend over there. Or perhaps you would deliver it for me and then ask *her* for a dance? I'm certain she dearly wishes to dance tonight." The two appeared torn, apparently attempting to choose between Iviana and the stunning blonde.

"Well…" started the one.

"I suppose I could—" interrupted the other.

Taking up a dessert dish, the first ended with, "I would be happy to aid you in this quest, my lady. I hope to meet you again at a later hour."

With that, Iviana was free of them. She quickly unhooked her dress and sat herself on a cushioned bench in the refuge of her dark corner. This was not turning out to be as simple as Merlow had said it would be. She was contemplating what she would do for the remainder of the evening when a presence appeared beside her.

Iviana turned in time to see the popular blonde, to whom she had just sent the eager men with the cake, sit beside her.

"My dear girl," began the woman." I fear I must

tell you I *loathe* cake."

Iviana had no words with which to respond, so sat with her mouth gaping.

"Oh, do close your mouth, you wondrous thing. It is only me."

"Wh—who?" Iviana asked, convinced this woman had her confused with another.

The woman ignored her and pointed to a gentleman who was dancing with an affluent looking woman. "You know, that man over there has been staring at you from the moment you entered the room."

Iviana squinted to where the woman had pointed and realized it was Sir Loric. Oh, how was she to avoid him? Still, that trouble was secondary to the affluent blonde speaking with her on such familiar terms. "I beg your pardon?" Iviana muttered.

"I pardon you," was the blonde's reply. "Oh, I suppose you can't tell who I am. We met only a few weeks back when I was, I'm sorry to say, in the form of a beastly wolf."

Iviana gazed into the woman's face and blinked. "Chamaeleo…"

"Hush, dear. There is reason I am not wearing my usual face. I am in this house for a purpose and there are those who must not know my true identity. I really haven't time to explain now, for the young man who has been staring at you is coming this way. I'll do you a favor and seize him for the next dance before he can get to you. I've noticed you're avoiding partners. If I were you, I would simply escape into the room behind that door over there before the staring man has rid himself of his next partner. You'll find a couple of friends hiding in there, but I must speak to you sometime before you leave this house."

Iviana spared only a moment to agree and thank the blonde Chamaeleo before moving purposefully to the door and stepping through the threshold. Both surprised and delighted, she walked freely up to the young men seated upon a large piano.

"Darist! Marquen! What are you doing in here?"

"More than likely we're here for the same reason as you," Marquen began easily. "We don't find the scene on the other side of that door to be our taste."

"I'm glad I'm not the only one," said Iviana. "The others look as though they've done this sort of thing every day of their lives."

"My friend, you look enchanting this evening," Darist commented. "Why aren't you dancing?"

"I don't know how," she told him. "I don't suppose the two of you do either."

"Not a step," Darist agreed.

"Well, this is a lovely enough room in which to enjoy a party," Iviana said happily. "The music is clear enough and there is a table of food only a few feet from the door. I expect we're going to have a grand time."

Darist nodded his agreement and began to jig about the room. "And I see no reason why my common dancing shouldn't be acceptable here," he said, casting a silly smile upon his friends. The tune outside was upbeat and Marquen chuckled at the sight of him, clapping his hands in time with the music. Iviana burst out laughing and was about to send a teasing comment when he took hold of her arm and swung her around in his arms, pulling her about the room.

"As you see, Marquen," said he. "Ivi is most enraptured with my style of dance." Iviana, trying to reply through her giggling, was swung around the room while Darist continued, "I am beginning to think it is how I capture the hearts of so many." Iviana was in a fit of laughter when he called, "Marquen, come down from that throne and grace us with a jig of your own." At last, he freed Iviana and urged her to clap with him while they waited for the show Marquen would give them.

Now the man who saw much had plenty of experience dancing in the solitude of his hills where only the Great One could see him, but Iviana was more delighted than she could express as she watched him move about the room like a mad man.

"It's the best dancing I've seen yet," Darist called laughingly.

Eventually, the three joined hands and circled the room, making themselves sick with dizziness. Iviana finally pulled herself away and fell unfashionably into the nearest chair.

"Oh, you two have to stop. I can't take anymore laughing," she cried.

Darist and Marquen exchanged wry grins and stomped about together until the music ended. The three bellowed merrily as the duo dropped in a worn heap upon the floor.

∞13∞

THE DOOR TO the room swung open and Loric was revealed, standing taller than his height should have permitted. "What goes on in here?" he inquired, attempting to keep his voice bright, but unable to completely mask his disdain for the giggling duo of men lying on the floor.

"We're in hiding," Iviana replied easily from her less than comely position in the chair.

"Why on earth do you hide, my lady?" he asked.

Iviana blushed and stood to her feet. "Loric," she said, "I cannot dance." Iviana was amazingly pleased at having finally admitted the fact to him.

Loric appeared surprised, but didn't miss a beat. "That is quite all right!" he exclaimed. "I am certain I could lead you through most of the dances, if you'll permit me." There was something in his tone that hinted a refusal would not be affably met—

something a little along the lines of agree or regret it.

Though Iviana couldn't be certain she had read him correctly, her face grew hot. She had no interest in attempting to follow the steps of a man she barely knew, but he was the son of the duke of Floresbury. Could she deny him? She hunted for a reply that wouldn't offend, but couldn't find one. The realization she would have to consent stole over her just as the door was again thrown open by a vivacious party of four. Necoli informed that his grandmother had revealed their hiding place and they had come to draw them out.

When no one spoke for a few moments, the newcomers recognized the tension not only emanating from Loric and Iviana, but from Darist as well, who was beginning to realize he did not care for this son of the duke, sixth heir to the throne.

Flynn, as much the gallant hero as ever, sauntered over to Iviana and hooked her hand through his arm. "Ivi, I don't care what you say; you're going to have a dance with me whether you like it or not."

Under normal circumstances, Iviana would never have permitted this, but there Loric stood, awaiting her reply, and it occurred to her she wouldn't mind if she never had to speak to the man again. She sensed something terribly unkind in him and did not wish to make herself vulnerable to it.

Besides, if she was going to look silly, she would rather do it with Flynn.

"If you insist," she replied as if she must not refuse him. She hoped this would help soften the blow for Loric.

"Flynn, your timing is impeccable," said Iviana after Flynn had escorted her out.

"I rather thought so myself," he replied. "I couldn't help noticing the way that man watched your movements about the ballroom. I don't think I care for him, myself."

"I don't believe I do either. I'm so grateful to you for stealing me away. Oh, but just look at the dessert table over there. I've only had one slice of cake, Flynn; let's go and get some."

"Oh, no, you don't," said Flynn, blocking her escape to the table. "I told you I was going to make you dance and that is what we are going to do."

"But I thought you only said that to help me get away from Loric."

"Correct, but that isn't to say I didn't fully intend on making you follow through. We can't have you making a liar of me."

He proceeded to pull her to the center of the room as Iviana attempted to fight him. "Flynn, don't you *dare*. I'm going to look like a fool in front of all these fine people."

As Flynn took hold of one of her hands and placed her other on his shoulder, he tried desperately to hide his amusement of her attempts to flee him.

"I've got a sword back in my room, my friend, and I know how to use it," she threatened through gritted teeth as he pulled her into the dance.

Flynn laughed freely, unable to stop himself. "As do I, but I believe the last time we met with swords, I had to spare your life. You may not be so lucky next time."

With flushed face, Iviana argued until she realized she was doing the very thing she had been claiming she couldn't. She was dancing. Not as gracefully as the other women, but she was pleased, just the same.

When the dance was completed, Flynn escorted Iviana to where the group of her friends were chatting together. Darist and Marquen had apparently been dragged from their hiding place and forced to mingle with the rest of them.

"Not too shabby," Darist commented to Iviana when she stood beside him.

"I thank you, sir," she replied with a curtsy.

"You see, Ivi," said Nimua, very pleased indeed. "It wasn't as terrible as you thought, was it?"

Iviana scowled at Flynn, but admitted she had enjoyed it.

"I always say the most enjoyable dances are with unwilling partners," Flynn said laughingly before turning to Brenna and adding, "Now, as I doubt our dear Seeker will take another turn with me just now, I don't suppose you're free for this next one?"

Nimua and Necoli followed them, leaving Iviana with Darist and Marquen.

"So they pull us out here only to leave us while they dance with one another," commented Darist.

Marquen chuckled his agreement, but replied with a yawn, "Our little party in the room back there was enough for me. I'm going to retire," and made his exit.

To Iviana's surprise, the remainder of the affair was enjoyable. She and Darist stood watching all that went on and laughing over small, humorous events that took place. For instance, Nimua tripped once or twice and was only saved from falling on her face by Necoli's swift retrievals and Flynn nearly spilled a drink down his front.

During an extremely elegant dance, Iviana commented that Nimua and Necoli looked well together, but kicked herself afterward, wondering if it hurt him to see Nimua with another.

"Darist?"

"Hm?" he replied tiredly.

"Do you mind that Nimua is with Necoli so often?"

Darist looked surprised. "Not at all. I'm glad she's happy."

This pleased Iviana, but she struggled to believe him. "But...Darist?"

"Yes, Ivi."

"Did you not have feelings for her?"

Darist was thoughtful. "Yes, of course I did, but when she told me she didn't have feelings for me, I realized I was glad. I guess my affection, of that sort, had faded."

Iviana heard in his tone that he spoke truly and was grateful. She loved Nimua and Darist and was happy their close friendship hadn't been marred. "Then you're still friends?" She wanted to make certain.

"Of course we are. We've been friends since we were kiddies. A little thing like our not wanting to get married can't change that."

With that, Iviana was content.

Periodically throughout the evening, there were those who ventured to ask Iviana for a dance, to which she responded with a series of excuses...at

Darist's expense.

"I'm afraid I cannot accept," she told one man. "My brother, here, is feeling faint and I must remain with him until he's better." Darist choked on his drink when first he heard this, but later looked forward to the men coming along to beg her for a partner, if only to hear what outrageous excuse she would contrive.

Darist also received attention from single and married women alike, though only a few were brave enough to ask him if he would take a turn with them. To these, Iviana also made his excuses.

"I am certain he would be pleased to dance with you if he could, my good lady," she would say, "but, you see, he is secretly engaged to a foreign princess and has promised he will dance with none but her until they are married."

Darist offered the ladies a regretful expression, but was each time surprised by the response it received. For the women, instead of losing interest, looked at him with new eyes. That this man was not only engaged to a princess, but had made so romantic a gesture made him a hero and they remained by his side until torn away by mothers, husbands or gentlemen wishing to dance. It wasn't long before Darist was the talk of the room, along with his faithful lady companion who remained by his side that he would not have to endure his not being able to dance alone.

Nimua had not heard these rumors, however, when she took Darist by the arm and tricked him into dancing with her. Necoli stood near, to make certain he could not escape her, and soon the women who had looked on him with delight scorned not the man that had broken his vow, but the angelic girl who had gotten him to dance. Nimua was quite popular after this—almost as popular as Chamaeleo—for every man who knew she was the only maiden in the room who had procured a dance from the fiancé of an enchanting, foreign princess— who was now rumored to be the daughter of the richest ruler on Kierelia's borders—now viewed her as a woman of great worth.

After the dance, Darist returned to Iviana's side in triumph.

"That was well done," Iviana lied.

"I know very well I looked ridiculous, but at least now I can tell Marquen that I did what even *he* would not do."

In the early hours of the morning, when the ball was nearing its end, many, if not most of the guests had cleared the ballroom. It was only those that had rooms in the castle who remained. Darist and Iviana were extremely tired, but had grown sillier with their drowsiness and enjoyed themselves all the more. When the waltz that Iviana had previously danced with Flynn was played again and only a handful of pairs were on the floor, Iviana dared Darist to take a turn with her. Her dare was received with a further dare that, if he accepted, she would not follow through. Eventually, the two were on the floor, and to the great pleasure of their friends, danced terribly together.

At the completion of their dance, Iviana was yanked away from Darist to face whoever had taken painful hold of her. Loric loomed over her with all the pride that a sixth heir to the throne could muster, informing he would have his turn with her as he twisted her into dancing position.

Earlier, Loric had attempted stealing her away for his much desired dance, but every time he was spotted nearby, Iviana and Darist had casually moved elsewhere. Now that Iviana was being mercilessly pushed and turned into the foreign moves of the dance, she realized she had driven this man into quiet fury.

With no other choice, Iviana tried desperately to keep up with whatever movements were expected, but unable to do so, Loric grew all the more irritated. Iviana thought the maddening twisting and turning would never end until, almost thankfully, he jerked her in such a way that her ankle turned painfully and she dropped to the floor.

Iviana searched for any breaks or sprains and tried desperately not to shed tears in front of Loric, who only stared down at her as though she was a clumsy child. It was screamingly apparent Sir Loric of Floresbury was not as charming as he had previously appeared.

As Iviana's comrades rushed to her side, Loric bent down and took possessive hold of her hand.

"I'm terribly sorry," he said in his old, pleasing way. "Allow me to help you to your feet. There are only a few steps left."

Iviana glared up at him in angered astonishment as she realized the tyrant expected her to finish the dance. *What a great, blasted fool!* she cried inwardly. As Iviana glared up at him, Flynn bent down and removed Loric's hold on her hand, silently taking it into his own.

"Oh, Iviana, are you alright?" cried Nimua.

Iviana turned her gaze from Loric to answer, "I'll be alright. It was a bad twist, but it's not sprained." She felt almost numb, for she was overwhelmingly angry at the unfeeling oaf beside her. She doubted he had any heart at all and would surely have made her miserable had she followed the advice of others. Whatever pleasing manners he had shown her previously had been for his own gain, whatever his purpose had been.

Darist placed his arm around Iviana, making ready to carry her out, but she was not accustomed to being transported around like a helpless doll in front of creatures such as Loric. Instead, she instructed Darist and Flynn to help her stand and proceeded to limp out of the room.

The fool who was Loric followed, however, and asked if he might enjoy her company later that afternoon. With that, Darist and Flynn disappeared from Iviana's side.

On her way out, Iviana overheard Darist say in a tone she had never heard him use before, "If you, Loric, son of a duke, ever go near that young lady again, you will learn well what gift the Great One bestowed on me."

Of course, Loric could not know all that Darist's threat entailed, but Iviana bit back a laugh as she imagined the fear it had inspired in Sir Loric, son of the duke of Floresbury, sixth heir to the throne and extremely eligible bachelor of Kierelia.

∞

The following day Iviana was sought and found by the blonde Chamaeleo. Though Iviana knew by now the blonde standing before her in the stables was, in fact, Chamaeleo, it took a moment for it to register. She simply looked nothing like the woman she had previously met.

"Ah, Cham—er, no...what am I supposed to call you?"

"Lady Mildred."

"Who are you, then, when you're a wolf?"

Chamaeleo looked about, searching for anyone who might have heard. "Hush, dear...I'm still Chamaeleo then..."

Iviana stifled a giggle, not entirely certain why this was funny. "Well, would you mind explaining why you're Lady Mildred just now?"

Chamaeleo nodded and motioned for Iviana to follow. When they came to a secluded corner of the courtyard, she began, "It's a long story. I can't tell you everything now, but I will begin with the beginnings of my trouble in this world.

"As you know, I am a Shifter, but I'm also a Seer. Like you, I have been given more than one gift, but that is not important in this tale. Some years ago, more than I care to tell, I was given a place in one of the lesser castles east of here. I was hired on as a washer woman and eventually became servant to the lady of the house. One night, I had a dream warning that the lady's life was in danger. The next day, I urged the woman to leave with me. By this time, we had become very close, so she consented even without explanation. Together we visited the household of a friend of hers and when we returned to the castle, it was discovered another of the servants had taken advantage of the empty, luxurious bed and been killed while she slept there. That was when my ability was discovered.

"After that, I was no longer servant to the lady, but deemed wise woman of the earl who lived in that fortress. I was more than happy to offer the man whatever information the Great One offered, but word of my ability spread. It wasn't long before the king himself ordered the earl give me up that I may work as the royal wise woman—this was our current king's father, King Curiel. At the time, I was greatly honored and my ego fairly puffed. I was foolish.

"King Curiel was careful at first. He asked simple things. Of course, I see now he was only testing my ability, careful that I was not using it to manipulate my way into power. When at last he was convinced I was a true prophet, well...that is when the trouble began. I won't delve into the details, but I became his pawn—at least for as long as I put up with it. I ran away from him.

"I admit I was surprised when the whole kingdom was unleashed in search of me. I had been more important to him than I realized. Luckily, He did not know of my shifting. It was easy enough to change forms, but, the fool I was, I began to prophesy again. My seeing abilities are very...keen. I suppose my style was altogether too recognizable, for it became common knowledge, after a time, that I—called Listar at the time—was able to change my shape. More likely than not, I was careless and changed form before someone.

"They call shifting witchcraft here, of course, though why my seeing is not viewed as such is a question. King Curiel despises witches, so to call me one, he would have had to kill me and he didn't want that—still doesn't want it, for he yet refuses to call me a witch himself. It is only the rest of the kingdom. Well, most of it...not all."

Iviana knew too well how quick the Kierelian people were to accuse one of witchcraft. She did not say so, however. She was too interested in what she was hearing to interrupt. Learning of Chamaeleo's experiences made her realize they had a good deal in common.

"Goodness, I really am trying to make a long story short," Chamaeleo continued. "There is yet so much more—this is, in fact, only a glimpse..." She escaped into some memory before, "I'm sorry...where was I? Ah, you see, in many of my shapes, I am on the run because of the things I'm known to do in them. But the shapes I may take are innumerable. I am not always safe as Chamaeleo, but it is my preferred form and it is lesser known than some of my other guises. This Lady Mildred character, I invented some time ago. I use her to gain information. There are those in Kierelia that I work with for the secret good of the land, so I masquerade as the daughter of a lord when I must live among the rich. I am here now to check on a few of the guests staying with your friends. Besides, I promised I would find you all. It so happened you led me to the very place I needed to be."

Iviana studied Chamaeleo, wishing she could learn every detail there was to know. She was fascinated by her, but she could see this was all Chamaeleo intended to share. She only hoped they would meet again and she would learn more one day, but Iviana said none of this. "You seem to enjoy being this enchanting Lady Mildred."

Chamaeleo laughed. "I am a little vain and I do enjoy prancing about as a beautiful, young woman. Besides, it helps to be well-liked when you're after information. I simply make it my mission to be esteemed by everyone as Lady Mildred so every line of gossip is open to her."

"That makes sense," Iviana hesitated, then continued, "I am curious, however, as to why you needed to speak with me."

Chamaeleo's eyes widened slightly. "Of *course*. How silly of me. Here I was supposed to relay a message to you and I sit here telling you my life story. I *am* getting old." She thought a moment before shaking herself and turning toward Iviana. Slowly, she began, "I sense something is coming for you, Iviana—perhaps already here. I felt it the moment I saw you on the road weeks back. Something has been unleashed to find you, something...dark."

"Why, what do you mean?" Iviana asked, at once concerned.

Chamaeleo shook her head. "I do not wish to frighten you, my dear. Only to warn you. And...and to remind you of this: the power of mere words uttered from the tongue of a child of the Great One contain great power."

Iviana stared back at her and nodded. "Yes. Naphtali always told me that. But I don't have Flynn's power. I'm not a Speaker."

Chamaeleo shook her head. "Haven't you learned yet? Eh, oh well. You will eventually. It's your destiny to learn it and to share it. Until then, just keep...*breathing*."

Iviana huffed, but she understood. Just as she understood Chamaeleo would share no more than she already had. Looking into the eyes of the fair woman, she said, "I still can't believe you're Necoli's grandmother. *Oh*...oh, dear..." Iviana suddenly realized Chamaeleo may not yet know what happened to Necoli's parents. She didn't know whether his father or mother had been her child, but they were both gone.

"What is it, Iviana?"

Iviana put her hand over her mouth, wishing she had not burst out. This was a family affair—not hers. "I..." she muttered.

"Come, my dear. Whatever it is, spit it out."

"Has Necoli told you?"

Chamaeleo looked into her eyes. "Told me what?"

"About his parents…"

"What of them?"

Iviana closed her eyes. "Perhaps you should ask him."

"Iviana, whatever it is, it's alright to tell me. His parents are my very good friends."

Opening her eyes, Iviana asked, "Friends?"

"Well, yes. Oh, I suppose you couldn't know. I am not his grandmother by blood. I am sort of his adopted grandmother. I've known his parents for a long time and Necoli needed someone to look out for him from time to time, so we became very close. He's always called me his grandmother and half the time I forget it's not by blood. Now, please, Iviana, tell me, are they alright?"

"Well…" Iviana began. "They're with the Great One. They're no longer living."

"No…" Chamaeleo's eyes were pricked with tears. "Tell me what has happened."

Iviana shook her head. "No, I'm sorry, Chamaeleo, but that I just won't tell. You have to speak with Necoli. I know I seem unfeeling, but—"

"It's alright, Iviana. I should speak to my grandson. Besides, I did nearly the same thing to you when first we met."

Iviana recalled the first conversation they'd had

and how this woman had disappeared. "Oh, you were the little girl with the basket on her head!" she suddenly realized. "You never disappeared at all! That was a terrible trick. Oh, but that was different. I'm sorry I was the one to tell you."

"I'm glad you told me. I don't know if Necoli would have without my probing. He doesn't share much lately and this...he would not have spoken of on his own, I think. Oh, but I suppose you know him. Perhaps he has changed? He certainly seemed different last night."

"He is different," Iviana affirmed. "I'm ashamed to admit I didn't like him at all when we met, but Nimua was right; there is more to him and it has begun to show."

"I can't tell you how glad I am to hear it. If he has lost his parents, I am certain he has much to deal with. But I see he has finally found some worthwhile friends."

Iviana smiled. "He has. I've invited him to continue our journey with us and I hope he will settle down with the others when we return to the Isle of Dragons."

"Mmm, I'd be nervous he wouldn't remain with you, but I have seen him with your lovely friend. She seems a treasure."

"Nimua? Yes, she is the best girl I know."

"Then I hope my grandson deserves her."

Her comment set Iviana thinking. She remembered her first meeting with him—earring, attitude and all—and then remembered the times she had seen him since, including the conversation they had the night of the banquet and finally last night at the ball. He had changed a great deal in a short amount of time. The ability to change for the better was an attractive characteristic. It showed humility and an openness of heart.

"You know, I think he does," she finally replied and was happy to recognize her dear friend's heart was in safe hands after all. Then she thought about Brenna and Flynn and realized three of her closest friends were likely to be married soon.

"Why did your face change just then?" Nimua asked as she approached.

Iviana leaped in her seat. "Oh, Nim...where's Chamaeleo?"

"I don't know. I haven't seen her all day."

"Well, she was just here. I didn't see her go."

"That's odd."

"Where did you come from?"

"I was walking and saw you sitting here alone. You looked perfectly happy and then your expression changed."

"Oh. I was just thinking about how quickly life can change. You've really got to relish every moment, haven't you? Because it can vanish in a blink."

"Good gracious, what are you talking about?"

"Not vanish...I suppose. But life is life isn't it? It keeps moving forward." Iviana shook her head as if to clear it and stood to her feet. "Come on, Nim. Lets go find the others and decide what is to be done about our quest."

❧14☙

IVIANA AWOKE WITH a start. Gasping from whatever nightmare she had endured, her eyes scanned the room. She wasn't entirely certain what it was she searched for, but sensed something near, watching, waiting. Whatever it was, it filled her with dread.

Iviana sat upright in bed and glared about the room with new vigor. Not even Merlow was about this early. Bolting from her bed, she began to peek under furniture and behind curtains as it occurred to her she had felt something similar several times throughout her journey, but had not wanted to face it.

Iviana felt it may be connected to the dream she'd been having just as she'd awoken. Perhaps these feelings were born entirely of that dream and she need not be anxious. Still, she completed her useless search and fought to remember it. Reaching into her memory, it felt as if she was grasping for something she had actually lived and, whatever it was, it gripped her with its importance. Even so, it was hidden from her, cloaked beyond the fabric of her conscious mind.

"Go! Run!" The words echoed within, reaching into her memory from that dream reality, calling her away, yet urging her to remember.

Flames, screaming, anguished sobbing, people were fleeing and then...

She'd been standing in an unknown town. The sky was black, but the streets were filled with people celebrating some special occasion. It was the fifty-year anniversary of the town having been officially formed, if what she gathered from a conversation she was overhearing was correct.

At first, she thought to hide her obvious eavesdropping as she attempted to learn where she was, but soon learned she was dreaming, for she was ignored by all—all except one little girl, she realized. She noticed the child who couldn't have been older than five study Iviana curiously, though it was evident she could not see her clearly enough to understand what she was seeing. Still, the child sensed something amiss. This knowledge flustered

Iviana, for this was either a strange dream or she had somehow transported to this town in her sleep.

At last, she called to the girl, testing if she could be heard by her, if not seen. But the moment her greeting was spoken the girl's eyes grew wide with fright and she ran after her older sisters.

Iviana watched her until a group of young people came giggling in her direction. For a moment, she thought they had seen her, but they proceeded to step easily through her being, an unnerving sensation she learned wasn't worth repeating. As a couple moved in her direction, she quickly stepped aside and began down the road.

Moving about unseen, it occurred to her this situation felt familiar, but her attention was soon diverted by a group of street-dancers displaying their talent for the surrounding audience. Their movements were beautiful, fluid and other-worldly, as if inspired by dreams. Perhaps that wasn't far from the mark considering she was most likely doing just that. Still, the dancers, clothed in dazzling garments, would have been a great pride to a town of that size and it was apparent the people appreciated their talent.

Despite the fact Iviana did not know where she was, why she was there or if she was only dreaming, she began to relax and enjoy observing the town's jubilation. When Iviana noticed a light shooting through the sky, glowing beautifully above the nearby forest, it seemed to suit the evening's atmosphere. But with each breath it drew closer and she watched it more diligently. Soon, others began to take notice and were pointing in the direction of the light as it blinked in and out of existence, like fire being lit and snuffed out over and over. Suddenly, the trees below blazed violently with that same light.

Iviana had never seen anything like it except...when Tragor had burned the evil sorceress, Aradia, to ashes. This could not be Tragor, but as the form manifesting the fiery light drew nearer, it was apparent a creature hated by all, a dark dragon, was shooting toward them like a fiery star falling from the heavens.

There was sudden shouting as others began to recognize the form.

"Go! Run!" someone called, startling the dancers from their performance as they realized they had lost their audience.

Iviana's mind scrambled for what to do as the dragon's mighty form threw its first flaming burst. Fortunately, though it sent the people scattering in terror, no one appeared to have been injured. Even so, a roof and a few nearby trees had caught fire and the dragon was rounding toward them again.

As the dragon drew near, Iviana reached for her sword and found it was not at her side. She had no time to search for another, for the small girl who had taken notice of her earlier stood paralyzed within the dragon's line of fire. Without debating whether what she was about to do was possible in her invisible state, she dived for the girl and covered the child with her own body as flame flooded over the two.

As the dark creature returned for yet another assault, Iviana stood and shouted for the nameless girl to follow her out of the town and into a small crop of bushes some distance away from the chaos.

With great relief, Iviana found the child had managed to follow her by the sound of her voice. "Stay here," she told her, but as the girl's eyes searched for the source of the sound, Iviana knew she could not see her, that she could not understand what was happening. Indeed, Iviana did not understand it herself, nor did she understand why she had not felt the sting of the fire or how it had not passed through her and over the girl.

Iviana turned in time to see the dragon land within the center of the town and at once set off to see what could be done, but as she should have drawn nearer, the scene faded from her sight until she awakened in her bed.

"No!" Iviana cried as she recalled the last.

Clinging to a bedpost, she breathed heavily, sweat dripping from her temples. It was as if, in remembering it all, she had lived it over again. But it had been a *dream*. It *must* have. Yet, she could not quench the anxiety building within. Even the atmosphere pricked and teased, revealing *something* was afoot. She only prayed it wasn't related to the nightmare in any way. Still, she could not help wondering if it had been a vision sent by the Great One. If so, how could He have made her endure witnessing another horrifying scene in which she was not allowed to aid those in need?

Filled with urgency, she swiftly dressed before exiting the room, knowing full well how cross Merlow would be that she had left before breakfast. But this was too important. She needed to determine if there was any real reason for her to feel as she did or she wouldn't have a moment's peace.

As Iviana moved through the halls of the fortress, she passed groups of strangers whispering about some pressing matter. This did not serve to ease her. Rather, her heart beat faster with every step. At last, she glimpsed Flynn through the threshold of a quiet room.

"Flynn!" she cried. "What's going on?"

He pushed his hand through his hair and grasped the back of his neck. "There's a dragon—a dark one. Seems it's been leaving a trail of ravaged villages in its wake and appears to be headed directly for us."

Iviana gasped and shouted within. It simply could not be. Her stomach twisted itself into knots as she attempted to determine what it all meant, what her nightmare had been.

Knowing what had brought on the darkness of the creatures did not help either. Instead, it sent a shiver through her at the thought of meeting one. Some time ago, a number of dragons had been lured into demonic flames crafted with sorcery and been possessed by the daemons within the fire. Most had been defeated, but some yet remained.

Iviana had no doubts as to what she desired to do with this one. If anyone was going to go after the repugnant beast, it would be her.

"I think we should defeat it before it arrives," Flynn broke into her thoughts.

Iviana peered up at him. "I agree."

"After all, if you think about it, it was sort of our world's fault it happened at all...all that business with Aradia and your great-grandfather, you know.

Besides, I know a woman who's pretty good with dragons..."

"Not *dark* ones," Iviana reminded, "but you're right."

"Lets leave now, then. I don't want the others to find out what we're doing. There's no way they'd let us go without them and I don't want to bring them into this—especially since most of them don't know how to use a weapon."

"But you're fine with allowing me to accompany you?" Iviana queried with a raised brow.

Flynn shrugged. "You're the savior of dragons and damsels. There's no one I'd rather have by my side. Besides, you've got that tight-knit friendship thing with the Great One. We could use a little extra favor."

"So you're using me?" Iviana asked with a smirk.

Flynn chuckled. "Yes."

∞

A while later, they were waiting within the stables as a duo of horses were being prepared, but as Iviana watched, she realized they were readying a third. Looking about, she spotted Sir Retrom giving orders to one of the stablemen. He was dressed for battle.

"Retrom," Iviana began, "there's no need for you to go. We've already made plans to handle it."

"I'm the overseer of the villages that are currently burning," he said miserably. "I'm going."

"Please, Retrom," added Flynn. "I would feel much better knowing you were here with my sister. Suppose it gets past us? You will be here to defend your home."

Sir Retrom looked from one to the other numerous times. "You are capable, I know…Oh, alright. I agree to your going, but I'm not going to remain here. I'll gather some men and see what can be done for the villages that have been damaged. There will still be plenty of men left to defend the estate should it come to it. I wish you luck…and I thank you. Truly, I do." He looked to Flynn. "Make sure you tell my wife goodbye before you go."

That was the moment Iviana realized there was a fair chance they would not return, but she barely had time to register this before a dark creature of another sort was beside her.

"Who on earth do you think you are?" queried Loric, disdain dripping from his words.

"Excuse me?" replied Iviana.

"You think *you,* a woman, is capable of facing a

dragon? Have you confused yourself with the dominant gender? But, who am I kidding? Look at what you've got on. Don't you know it isn't seemly for a woman to be dressed as a man, Iviana? If that's your real name."

Flynn stepped in front of Iviana, fuming and ready to lop the head off this snake, but Iviana stepped around him and gestured she wanted to handle this on her own.

"What do you mean by insulting me this way? And why should the name I gave you not be my own?"

"Oh, you know perfectly well what game you've been playing at, dressing and acting as a noble when you're just a poor wood-witch. Yes, I did some digging into why you were wandering the castle the evening you woke me with your mopping. It seems one of the servants suspiciously recovered from the brink of death that night. And I don't suppose you noticed one of the kitchen servants used to live in FairGlenn, where our own little witch girl was born and raised. Tell me, my '*lady*,' did you really think I would marry you? Did you think I would not discover what you truly are? I am from the royal blood line. I cannot very well betroth myself to just anyone."

"That's enough, Loric," Iviana interrupted. She couldn't believe she had ever given this man a moment's thought as far as anything beyond friendship. She saw now what a trap she had been spared, but there were more pressing matters at hand and he was wasting her time. "I never planned on betrothing myself to anyone, let alone a blithering idiot such as yourself. And never once did I claim to be anything but what I am. It was your own shallow assumptions that got you into the little mess you created. Now, if you don't mind, I've—"

"Oh, come, come, you think I'm going to let you just trot away? I'm taking you to King Curiel so you will be imprisoned for the conniving witch you are."

He attempted to take hold of her wrists, but she had easily pulled out of his grasp when both Flynn and Retrom stepped between them.

"Not so fast, Loric," said Retrom. "I am more ashamed of you than I ever thought possible. You may consider our friendship as well as your welcome in this household finished, effective immediately. As far as Iviana is concerned, she is under my protection while she is within my land and I order you to keep your hands off her, else I will have you imprisoned."

Loric released a shocked, pathetic laugh. "Mark my words, *woman*," he called over Retrom's shoulder. "You may not want to plan on returning to this castle nor any civilized part of Kierelia, for that matter. I will have you hunted by the whole of the kingdom for the witch I know you to be...not that you're going to survive your dragon." He was suddenly pleased by the thought.

Flynn could take his pathetic threats no longer. He stepped forward and swung a swift hook to Sir Loric's protruding jaw. The only thing that kept him from following with another was Retrom and Iviana pulling him back.

"I mean what I said," Retrom called to Loric as he made a swift exit, holding his wounded jaw. "I want you *gone.*" When he was a safe distance away, Retrom and Iviana released Flynn. "I'm afraid Loric's threats are never empty," Retrom said regretfully. "He *will* have you hunted, whether or not you are on my land. And probably you as well, Flynn, now you've injured his prided jaw."

Flynn looked down at Iviana and said with sympathy, "You won't be able to return to FairGlenn." He knew what this meant to her.

"You won't be able to return to your sister," Iviana countered.

Flynn shrugged. "I might be able to manage a quick visit now and then. You've just lost your home."

"Touché," Iviana replied with a wry half-smile. "But I'll worry about that later. Just now, we've a dragon to slay."

∞15∞

THE CLOUDLESS SKY above was a piercing contrast to the atmosphere within the lowland as all sound was muted to the ears of the forms below—the only resonance the pounding of their own hearts. Iviana cast a meaningful glance to Flynn, relaying her feelings, but returned her attention to the dark dragon before them. Apparently, they were rendered to gawking, for this creature was grandly enormous—larger than any they had beheld. Deeply ashen in hue, it was truly ominous, every muscle of its body taut, its veins bulging and pumping wildly against its leathery epidermis. Even so, its chest moved languidly in and out, proving this meeting was of no significant consequence to the giant.

Over the course of their journey to this pivotal valley, Iviana had been forced to view the aftermath of what this epic brute had bestowed on the village from her dream. She would never have recognized it if not for the little girl who stood outside the door of what was likely her home. Though the town had certainly seen devastation, Iviana was surprised to find there was anything left of it at all. In fact, the home of the child still stood, the only damage a charred roof.

Iviana made her way up to the house and stood before the dainty child. As their eyes met, it was apparent the girl was attempting to work out why Iviana was familiar to her.

"Was anyone…was anyone killed?" Iviana asked.

The girl flinched at the sound of her voice, but shook her head quickly in response. "Only hurt."

Relief flooded over Iviana. "Were they wounded badly?"

"My uncle lost his arm, but everybody else is only hurt a little."

Iviana had wished she could remain to help the townspeople clean and rebuild, perhaps to heal those who would allow her, but knew she was needed far more elsewhere. Looking about at the ruined town, what she wanted in that moment was to avenge those wronged by the beast.

"What's your name?" Iviana asked the girl.

"Rosie," she replied shyly.

Iviana knelt before her.

"How would you feel about my making that nasty dragon pay for all this?"

Rosie looked quizzically into Iviana's face, but noted the strength she found there.

"I think everybody would like that....'specially my uncle."

Iviana stood with a grin. "You got it."

And the Seeker fully intended to be true to her word, but she had not anticipated the grand spectacle before her. Forcing herself to step further into the valley, the dragon studied them intently, openly and arrogantly reading them. Iviana felt the hairs on the back of her neck lift. She had felt something similar when she first met Tragor—an intelligence that reached beyond human capacity—but this was far more terrifying. It pierced her soul with a hundred eyes at once.

Iviana met Flynn's gaze again and nodded. The two gripped their swords and took a few steps closer, yet uncertain what was to be done with a mountainous dragon that did nothing but watch them. What was it waiting for?

As its uncanny gaze continued penetrating their confidence, Iviana began to sense it had been anticipating their arrival. It was apparent the dragon was not surprised by their sudden appearance in the valley. In fact, it was rather pleased, as if they had carried out just what the creature bid them. With that thought, Iviana's legs began to tremble.

Next thing she knew, a blast of blinding flame escaped the dragon's glowing jaws. She barely dodged the attack. Huffing and feeling as if she had awoken from some slow-motion dream-state, reality loomed before her in the form of this formidable enemy.

"Ivi, pull back!" Flynn called.

Iviana ignored him. She knew he regretted letting her come with him, but he had to know there was no way she would leave him—especially not if this dragon had truly been expecting them. If this was the case, the creature meant business and she meant to discover what it was.

Iviana charged the beast, her sword raised, but was forced to flee as fire flew toward her, narrowly missing its mark. Unbeknownst to Iviana and the dragon, Flynn stole the moment to attack and pierced the dragon's side. Almost as an unconscious reaction, the dragon's leg kicked Flynn against a nearby rock, sending stars to his vision. But this was all the reaction the wound produced, for the dragon did not slow nor stop to nurse its wound.

Torn between racing to Flynn's side and following his strike with another, Iviana darted behind another series of rocks to protect herself from the next inferno. Panting behind her shelter, she struggled to come up with a plan that would get them past the reach of the dragon's flame, but could see none if Flynn did not move soon. She could see him still sprawled against the rock, most likely unconscious.

Iviana realized the irony of the scene as she recalled her initial encounter with Flynn, when the two had fought over the life of another dragon. At that time, they had been enemies. Now, they were in agreement as to what should be done with this one; it was to be slain without mercy. It had just lay to ruin numerous towns, not to mention the lives that had been taken in the process. All this was done in an attempt to gain their attention. Yes, she knew it to be true...somehow. Perhaps the dove had whispered it into her spirit, but she was certain the dragon truly had called them to this place, in its way.

A large, black shadow loomed over Flynn's body and, though Flynn seemed to be gaining consciousness, Iviana knew the dragon would finish him. With no thought in her mind but ending its life before it could take the life of her friend, she flew forth headlong toward the dragon, who had incurred new anger from her not only for slaughtering innocent people in an attempt to reach her, but for daring to go after her unconscious friend. If she had to, she would give her life in an attempt to save him.

Upon seeing Iviana, the dragon's lips curled in triumph before releasing another burst of flame. This time, as Iviana fled, it followed. Within that smirk, Iviana realized she had reacted as the dragon had expected. She had fallen for its trap.

The fierce heat began to burn her flesh as it overtook her when she heard rather than saw the shadow of a large wave of water crashing toward her. As the water surged over her body, knocking her about mercilessly, all she could think was, *How?* As soon as it ceased coursing over her, she looked to the dry land from where it had come.

"Marquen?" she gasped.

He stood a few yards behind her with his arms held out as if he had just thrown the wave to meet the dragon's flame, but how he had accomplished this as well as found out where they would be found was beyond Iviana. They had asked Retrom not to tell the others of their pursuit.

Marquen nodded and sent another sourceless wave to meet the confused dragon's next attack. This time, the water reached the dragon's face and smoke seethed where it touched as if it burned. Watching impatient confusion replace the dragon's arrogance made Iviana smile just a little.

"Marquen, *how* are you doing that?" Iviana cried.

"Why do you think I lived on my hill? I'm a Swimmer as well as a Seer, among other things. My people aren't altogether in favor of one who has been blessed with multiple gifts, as you know, and I was the first. But there's much more to being a Swimmer than swimming. We can call upon water from the heavens, should we choose. As far as I know, however, I'm the only one to have discovered and made use of this." He said the last with a smirk, as if he had just revealed a favorite secret.

"Gracious, you're powerful," Necoli commented from behind Marquen. "Show me how you did that."

It was then Iviana realized the rest of their group had come after them. Though Iviana had been in agreement with Flynn in their not coming, she was suddenly grateful to have them near...so long as they kept away from the danger.

Danger. Why wasn't the dragon continuing to attack?

Flynn, who had obviously revived from his blow

to the head, shoved Iviana out of the way of another strip of fire. The heat scorched her eyebrows and curled the hairs on her arms, stunning her into shame as she inwardly kicked herself for losing focus. Where was her head?

Iviana could hear Nimua shouting at Necoli to let her go to them. Iviana was grateful he wasn't letting her. Nimua needed to stay far away if Iviana was going to face this nemesis. Nimua was a weakness she did not need exploited.

Having somehow lost her sword in all the dodging, Iviana stole the blade from Flynn's hand and charged at the beast. She hoped if she could move fast enough she would be able to get the weapon into the creature before it could hurt her too badly.

More waves were sent to meet a number of the dragon's fiery attacks. These came from Brenna, who had apparently sought and found that part of her gift. *Good for you,* thought Iviana even as she was pelted by the water coursing toward the dragon. She preferred battering waves to dragon fire any day. Even so, it was growing difficult to draw her feet from the mud the water was creating and this slowed her attack. She only hoped the beast was too distracted by the waves to notice her.

When she had drawn quite near, however, the dark dragon took notice of her and charged, ramming her in such a way she could not reach its flesh with Flynn's sword. About to be trampled by the dark creature, Iviana stole her only chance of survival by taking hold of one of its scaly horns and pulling herself on top of the dragon's neck.

"Ivi, you *crazy dragon lady*, give me back that sword and I'll handle him before he's sent you to the Great One," Flynn shouted.

Iviana ignored him once again. She had a better chance now of harming the dark dragon. That is if she could do so without falling. Struggling to hang onto the backside of the beast's head, she heard Marquen and Flynn arguing over whether the waves would do Iviana more harm than good.

"Just do it!" she called to them.

Iviana was uncertain how much damage she could do before it succeeded in flinging her off and she wanted it weakened; water seemed to manage this. She wondered why this dragon was affected by water in such a way—as she had recently learned dragons can live within the water if they choose—but assumed the daemons within had transformed its natural state when they had taken the graceful creature and turned it into a maddened monster.

As she lay atop the flat side of Flynn's blade, clinging to the neck of the dragon with her arms and legs, she had to think up a plan.

I'm not doing much good if I can't get the sword out from under me without dropping it, she decided. *Though, at the very least, I'm preoccupying it from any further attack on the others.*

But the beast was angry and growing more so every moment. As Iviana clung to its flesh, its body temperature rose with its fury. Soon, Iviana's eyes watered from the powerful heat. She was very near losing her grip when she felt its head drop to the ground. Iviana dared a peek over the dragon's head and found Darist, who seemed to have taken hold of the dragon's muzzle, and used his anointed strength to pin it in place. The dragon's body was yet mobile, but there was not much it could do with its head in a vice.

"Ivi, do what you gotta do!" Darist called.

Iviana nodded, her skin burning against the dragon's. She sat up, legs gripped tightly around its neck. Having taken hold of the sword, she held it out above her head and in a breath had it stabbed into the neck of the dark dragon. Immediately, she was covered with steaming, hot blood and she flung herself from the dragon, crying in agony. The sword remained in place.

The dragon roared and desperately tore its head from Darist's grasp. Darist rolled away in time to miss being crushed beneath the raving creature. He, Flynn and Nimua raced to Iviana and attempted to wipe the sticky blood from her, but only succeeded in burning themselves. Iviana was crying out in pain when a rush of cool, clear water flooded over her. It was Necoli who supplied it, having finally succeeded in calling upon the Swimmer's water. Iviana reveled in the relief it supplied, but when she discovered the dragon still alive, rolling about in pain, it was almost too much for her. Exasperated she had given such a deep, vital stab, she wondered how it yet moved and breathed.

Next thing she knew, Flynn called out a battle-cry and ran toward the beast with Iviana's muddied sword. He had just reached the dragon when it sent a large blue flow of angry fire over him. Flynn just veered before it could engulf him, but not before half his body received burns. Still, he continued and was winding about after the dragon, pursued by flame.

"Flynn!" Iviana called. "Stop and let these Swimmers douse it in water first! Lets weaken it as best we can!"

Flynn obeyed and retreated. He was met with

Brenna's relieving water while Marquen and Necoli went after the beast, sending wave upon mighty wave over the dragon. The valley was a mess with mud and water as steam and smoke filled the air until the spectacle could no longer be seen by the watchers.

"Do you think they're alright?" Iviana asked fearfully, glaring into the blinding fog and glad Darist and Nimua were on either side of her.

"Should I go help?" Brenna asked.

"You probably wouldn't be able to find them in all this," said Flynn.

So the five waited, blindly gazing into the mess for some sign of what was happening.

At last, Iviana saw movement and gripped Darist's hand. *Please, let it be them,* she prayed. Her prayers were answered as Necoli came sauntering toward them, the steam thinning. B*ut where's Marquen?* Just as Necoli reached them, another form appeared in the fog. Necoli turned back expectantly, grinning when he saw Marquen.

"You think the beasty's dead?" he asked him.

Marquen shrugged. "One can hope. We can't be sure until some of this has lifted." He swatted the mist.

The group sat together, silently awaiting the

moment they would discover the fruit of their efforts. None said a word. They only sat praying and hoping their battle was at an end. But Iviana didn't feel right. For one, it had been too swift a victory. Secondly, there was an evil yet present in the atmosphere, carried by the dragon. She assumed it would flea with the death of its bearer.

"Did you see that?" Brenna asked fearfully.

Iviana and the others squinted.

"Ah...I saw it that time..." Flynn whispered numbly.

Iviana's stomach tightened. She was worn and lucky to be alive. This needed to be over; she did not want to lose anyone. But there was a seething figure in the fog, breathing so heavily it pumped the mist and smoke about. Slowly, the form drew closer until it stood before them at its largest height and looked down on them with piercing contempt.

"Did you really think it would be that easy?" a low, reverberating voice spoke out of the dark creature.

No, thought Iviana. *Just no. This is not alright.* She said aloud, "Dark dragon of old, state your business with us."

" *You* are what we seek," the dragon rumbled.

"Why do you seek us?" Iviana demanded.

275

"We seek Iviana the Chosen, the bane of our masters."

Iviana shivered and Nimua reached a protective arm around her.

"What do you want with Ivi?" shouted Darist indignantly.

"Huuush, strong man. We speak only to the wench."

Darist gripped Iviana's arm as if he feared she would sacrifice herself. Flynn, Brenna and Necoli drew behind her and placed protective hands on her shoulders.

"What do you want with me?" Iviana squeaked out. This news was a shock. She didn't mind facing a dragon and attempting to slay it, but the fact this dragon had sought *her* purposefully was terrifying.

"The prophesies," hissed the dragon. This time there were multiple voices of various tones within its reply.

Iviana did not know what secrets the prophesies contained and she was both confused and intrigued by this dragon seeking her because of them.

"What do you mean?" she asked the daemons within the dragon.

"We cannot allow you to fulfill the destiny that has been laid before you by the One. We cannot let you leave this valley."

"What trouble could I possibly be to you?" she asked, her last words almost a whisper as it set in she was speaking to the demonic realm. It was difficult to believe these daemons sought to destroy *her,* of all people.

The dragon scoffed insolently in its deep voice, "Stupid, little thing, you do not know what lies in your future, but you have done enough thus far. In truth, you were insignificant to us before you defeated our witch, Aradia. Since that time, we've been following you throughout your travels, gathering information. We know you cannot fulfill your destiny, but we've learned more. You're a seducer and a trouble-maker who has set out to destroy the principles the One has set by way of Latos within the Greater Archipelagos." It chuckled as it spoke, "You are called the *chosen one* and yet you move against the very One Who called you."

"That isn't true!" Iviana screamed in anger. "Those are rumors formed by others! They're lies!"

"Notice all the men you surround yourself with...recall the laws you've broken. The proof is before you all."

The creature's words were striking hard as these were things that had been stated some time ago and had haunted her. She had thought those old wounds abandoned, but they were torn anew as they were used against her.

As Iviana began to shake, the dragon continued, "You have been called a witch, yet you take the life of ours, you little hypocrite." Suddenly, the voices paused and continued softly, "Iviana, you've lost the only family you've ever known and now you live out your days alone in your little wood. You will always be alone, Seeker. Your kind belongs with us. We can grant you your life if you will join our family. We will raise you up to do great things. In truth, you are a gifted young woman and are meant for greatness. Indeed, we will spare you if only you will say the word."

Iviana stood to her feet, suddenly enraged. "You lying, *sniveling snake*," she cried. "You twist truth and threaten my life and then puff me up and ask me to join you? Well, I have news for you. I am never alone—not one single moment of my life. Even when my dear friends are not beside me, I am accompanied by the *Creator of Worlds*."

The creature shuddered as she continued, "If you're afraid of whatever the Great One plans for *me* to do, then I can only imagine *He* terrifies you. Look at you! Clinging to the insides of a dragon's empty soul that you might come after me. Why can you not come at me yourselves? Why do you send another to do your dirty work?"

The truth dawned on her, as if spoken in a still, quiet voice and she said in surprise, "You have no authority to come after me, do you? You cannot physically come for me without another being's vessel as your tool. Why don't you come out of that dragon and face me and my God, if you dare?"

The dragon stared down over the small young woman with its gigantic frame. Iviana glared back up, fully confident in the One who was with her. She waited, but still the dragon did not move and she grew impatient.

"You worthless fools!" Iviana mocked. "Why don't you come out of that dragon and go back to wherever you came from?"

The dragon backed away, its eyes revealing great fear. "No, please...we can't," the voices sniveled out.

"In the name of the Great One, *go now!*" Iviana commanded.

What followed was a thing none of them would ever forget. The dragon coiled and curled as if fighting against the daemons inside that were trying desperately to preserve their victim as they screamed in frustrated agony. Iviana was certain they must be heard even beyond the nearest village

The group watched as the daemons appeared to have released the body. Iviana felt the evil flee as the corpse of the dragon fell to the ground, its energy and life spent by the demonic spirits. Iviana looked at the large, grotesque creature and wondered what it had been before, but shook her head, unable to think about that now. In truth, she realized she had done it a mercy. It had lived under others' control far too long. There had been nothing left of itself by the time she had come upon it.

❧16☙

NUMBLY, they set up camp a few miles from the valley. They had done this often in their travels, but those past evenings seemed a lifetime ago. Most of them sat a few feet from the flames, close enough only for light and companionship—for comfort—for they were too burnt to seek warmth. In truth, the fire was hardly a comfort to anyone. It would be some time before it was.

It had been debated whether they should make the hours long journey back to the castle, but they were too weak. Besides, Iviana and Flynn knew they could not return. Instead, they ate ravenously of the few things that had been packed, as none felt up to hunting or gathering. They would eat well in the morning, but tonight they rested.

Iviana sat between Darist and Flynn, as the three

had endured the most burns and did not want to be near the fire. Iviana had treated their wounds, but it would take time for complete healing to occur. They sat in some discomfort, but were too exhausted to care.

Still, despite Iviana's physical pain and fatigue, she could not squelch her feelings of triumph. They had actually bested the demonic. She realized this most likely had not been the first nor would it be the last time she would encounter them, but after what had occurred today, she felt confident she had a Power greater than any they possessed.

When at last everyone retired to their makeshift beds, Iviana was restless, so she took into her hands the old book Bell had given her. The moon was full and bright, almost as gleaming as the one in the Greater Archipelagos; it was just enough for her to read by.

Iviana continued reading about the Anointed One, who went by another name in her book. She read for some time, taking in all this man had done and was amazed at the way he lived. He was fearless, it seemed. When at last she came to the portion that she had personally witnessed, when the man was to be crucified before a scoffing people, Iviana squinted as the words on the page began to glow. They glowed so bright she could not continue reading, though she tried with all her might to see past the light.

Finally, she closed the book, shutting out the light. She wondered if Bell had known the book would do this or if the book had ever done so before. She sat until her breathing had slowed and opened it again. When she simply looked upon the page, it did not glow. But when she began to read, the words shown bright once more. The longer she read, the brighter they became until she could see nothing but their light.

Iviana attempted to close the book, but there was nothing in her hand. Her vision cleared then, revealing she had been transported to the lakeside where weeks before she had walked across its misted surface into another world.

Peering over the lake and into the mist, she could not make herself cross. The painful scene she had witnessed the last time was too fearful for her to bare viewing again. Besides, she had already seen it. Why would the Great One want her to endure it again?

"*Do you trust Me?*" she heard the voice of the Great One whisper.

Iviana shivered and recalled the night He had supplied the healing for Merlow's friend, young

Doggins. He had not deserted her then; she would not desert Him now. She stepped upon the water.

Her crossing was the same as her prior journey, but when she reached the end, she stood at the bottom of a white stairway. There was nothing else—just the stairs in perfect white and there, on the first step, stood a man.

Gazing into his face, Iviana was awed by it. In his all-encompassing eyes was warmth. In his beaming, radiant smile was *home*. Filled with a sense of wholeness, she attempted to decipher why the man seemed familiar, but could not place him. All this she took in in moments.

At last, she stepped forward.

Who are you? her heart asked.

Gazing into her spirit with that brilliant smile, he replied, "I love you."

Iviana did not question the statement, but somehow understood it to be true. It was not romantic by worldly definition, but tender in the purest, truest, deepest sense.

The man said it again and then again, "I love you, I love you," until the words had finally gripped her heart.

He loves *me,* she realized. *But who* is *he?*

"I am the son of my Father and I am His right

hand," he told her. And just as he opened his mouth to speak his next words, Iviana realized who he was. "*I am the Anointed One.*"

Iviana blinked up at him. "But I watched you die!" she cried. Tears pricked her eyes as she recalled what she had seen.

"I know. I saw you there," he said warmly. Then he added with the touch of a smirk playing at the ends of his mouth, "You tried to rescue me."

Iviana frowned. "But I couldn't."

The Anointed One nodded. "I know very well. I stopped you."

This confused her greatly. "Why?" she asked breathlessly.

"I am the son of the Great One. It was my destiny to die on that hill."

Iviana was no closer to understanding. "Yet, you live…"

"I do. You see, what you saw was a very deep moment in history. What you do not know is I rose again, fully alive, days later."

Dumbfounded, she asked, "*How?*"

The Anointed One smiled. "Will you sit with me?"

Iviana looked about to discover she was in a fragrant, glowing garden. Blossoms of various hues bloomed perfectly everywhere she looked, the greens piercing and glorious. She looked to where the Anointed One gestured to a beautifully ornate bench.

Taking a seat with him, she asked, "Where are we?"

"Eternity."

Iviana did not doubt it and though she had never in her life heard the word used as a place, she understood it.

"Ivi," he said, taking her hands in his. There was genuine emotion in his voice as he continued, "You're in pain." Iviana made ready to protest, but suddenly recognized he was referring to the pain in her heart. "Oh, sweet Ivi, you have been wounded by the people of your worlds. You have been rejected, judged, lied about and you have lost your family."

Iviana held back tears as she acknowledged the issues she had been trying to ignore. They had been causing her pain for some time. She had been sheltered and loved by Naphtali and her innocence protected. As she grew and learned the ways of others, that innocence within her fragile heart had been wounded and corrupted. She had never shared these pains with anyone, but this man knew them well. As he gazed deeply into her teary eyes, he saw everything and she knew it. Drawing a shaky breath, she waited for what this man, who loved her, would say.

"I, too, was abused, mistreated and...mistrusted," said he.

Iviana recalled what she had seen that day. They had been only the last moments of his life and they had been horrific.

"I know," she replied, remembering how disfigured he had been. Now her tears were shed for *him.* "Why were such unspeakable things done to you? Why did those people have such terrible hatred in their hearts?"

"I am the Lamb," he said simply. "I was sent into the world to rescue it. I was sent to save *you.* The Dark One, who is the stealer of innocence and the author of lies, came to steal and destroy those whom the Great One loves. He wounds their innocence that they may be imperfect before my Father so the Dark One can take them into his pit of shadows forever.

"I, who have existed through all eternity, went in human form to take upon myself the imperfections and sin of all people. Every evil, unclean thing, every curse, every disease, I wore into death. And I defeated the destiny the Dark One planned for you and replaced it with my own when I came back to life." He lovingly squeezed the hands he held and looked into her tear-stained face. "Iviana, I want to remove your pain. I want to restore your innocence. I want to rescue you, my precious love. Will you let me?"

Iviana peered back into his face. "If you died to save me," she began, "can I reject your offer and undo everything that was done to you in the past?"

The Anointed One laughed heartily, but when he ceased, his eyes were sad. "Iviana, do you not understand? My Father sent me in human form so I could save you. We love you so much. If you do not accept what I won for you, it will break my heart. Let me *win* you, will you, please?"

Iviana closed her eyes as tears streamed down her face. Her heart was filled with so much emotion she thought it might burst. What this man told her was the most beautiful thing she had ever heard or ever would hear. He was the sweetest person she would ever encounter. She never wanted to leave him.

"Oh, Anointed One..." she whispered, "I accept what you've done for me. I will let you into my heart. Rescue me, please, so I can be with you forever."

As her heart filled with him, she felt him reach her with his healing power and she began to weep over the wholeness he had given. As she wept, he drew her close and held her. As he stroked her hair, she knew she was done for. She was his, completely.

The Anointed One, still holding her close in his selfless sweetness, drew her to her feet. When she had cried all her tears, she looked around and realized they were standing at the bottom of the stairway again.

"Why are we here?"

"Iviana, one day you will be with me forever in my home...Paradise. Right now, I need to ask you for something. These stairs represent the journey I want to take with you before that time comes. I have a destiny for you, if you'll have it. There are things that must be done and the Great One and I need your help. You see, the Great One needs His warriors. If you can trust me, We would like you to carry the message of Our heart's cry and aid in a decision that must be made for the whole of the Greater Archipelagos very soon. Its outcome will determine the future of that land."

Suddenly, the dove appeared, landing on his shoulder. "This is my spirit. I would like to send him with you. Ivi...will you go back and do this for Us?"

Iviana did not have to think about it. "After what you have done for us and having learned the fate of those who do not know about it, how can I say no? If you'll lead me, I will do whatever it is you ask of me."

The son of the Great One gazed into her face with a beaming, affectionate grin and ran his hand through her hair. In the next moment, she was beside the lake. Iviana raced from the lakeside, allowing her Seeker's gift to lead her back to the camp. Her friends were sleeping and she shouted for them to awaken. She could finally reveal all now she had gained understanding of what she had seen so many nights ago. Her heart was filled with longing to share and she ignored Nimua's sleepy complaints, pulling stubborn Flynn from his bed.

With everyone assembled, she said, "I have found the lighted parchment." She looked over the faces of her friends around the dim campfire. They were fully awake now and ready to listen.

"Oh, go on, Ivi. Where is it? What does it say?" Brenna urged.

"It is bound within this book." Iviana held it up for them to see. "It tells of a great man...one I have just met."

"Oh, do tell me you've found a beau at last," said

Nimua.

Iviana grinned and shook her head. "He is the Anointed One, son of the Great One."

"Son of the Great One? The Great One has a *son*?" Marquen asked in astonishment.

"Yes," she replied, "and he is powerful and heroic, a true knight if ever I've met one. He...he is *home*, somehow. He is where I belong—I know it now. Someday, I will be with him forever, but I can't go yet because there are things I've got to do first—things *we've* got to do.

"I have found the lighted words and their message is this: we were dying in our imperfection, but he, the Anointed One, died in every way possible to defeat the ancient law of the Dark One that was to send us away from the Great One forever. It would have abandoned us in a place of terrible, unending shadow." She took a breath. "Do you understand? He died an excruciating death because he wanted to save the world...worlds...what I mean is all people. We were headed for a terrible fate, but did not know it. Now, he tells us—"

Necoli stood. "Has he saved me then, Ivi?" His eyes were red with tears not shed. "Can he save me? You don't know the things I've done. I need help. I need him...if he'll help me."

Iviana's face beamed. "Necoli, if you believe what I'm saying, your heart has already accepted him and you have been rescued. He can make you whole again and restore your innocence. Just talk to him—his spirit is with you now—ask him for forgiveness for whatever it is you are ashamed of. Necoli, you will be restored as I have been."

Necoli looked into Iviana's face and then into the heavens. He fell to his knees, closing his eyes. He was speaking to the Anointed One in his heart. As tears fell from his face, restorative light burst from his eyes, fingertips and toes. He stood and turned to the others. He did not speak, but his eyes glowed, infused with power.

Marquen stood then. He turned around and gazed into the starry night sky and spoke in his heart. Flynn smiled up at Iviana, then closed his eyes and did the same. Nimua, Brenna and Darist smiled too and let their hearts cry their acceptance unto the Anointed One.

As Iviana watched her friends under the glow of firelight, her heart was filled with destiny. A tune struck upon her lips and she began to sing a song of love unto her Great Friend. As she sang, Necoli took up a pair of spoons and began playing out a beat. Brenna gave her harmony once she'd learned the words. Marquen and Darist looked at one another and began to clap. Once Flynn and Nimua had the words, they sang as well. Each stood then and sang out the overflow of their hearts.

Soon, Marquen began to dance freely and was joined by Darist. Iviana leaped about, so filled with destiny she could not contain it. Nimua and Brenna laughed and then took hands to join in the dancing. As the music poured from them, the air was filled with thick qualities. A presence was making itself known. Iviana laughed, knowing full well whose it was. Nimua and Marquen saw flashes of wings and swords and heard the sound of other voices singing and instruments being played. The rest saw the effects of this as feathers floated about and glittering clouds of gold glistened in the deep atmosphere. In the midst of all this, the wounds and burns they had earned in battle against the dark dragon were healed.

The seven continued through most of the evening until the tune became a slow, easy one and they all lay in their beds. Their song continued until they were asleep and continued in their hearts thereafter. Iviana dreamed that night of days that were to come. Her understanding was not yet complete, but she knew the time was coming when her life would be as she had never dreamed possible.

FROM THE AUTHOR

I know there are many books out there to choose from, so I would like to personally thank you for following Iviana's journey in the Seeker's Trilogy. If you enjoyed this book, please consider leaving a review to let like-minded readers know they might enjoy it too. To connect with me, visit any of the following sites:

CassandraBoyson.com

Facebook.com/CassandraBoyson

Twitter.com/CassandraBoyson

Or find me on Goodreads.com